Born in 1956, Tom Walton spent most of his working life in the road haulage industry in a senior management role, and retired in 2019. He is married to Sue for the past 41 years. Tom has two grown-up children – his daughter is here in the UK with two sons, and his son lives in the Northern Territory, Australia, he also has two sons.

To all the campers and caravanners that made my weekends memorable.

Tom Walton

CAMPING CHRONICLES

AUSTIN MACAULEY PUBLISHERS™
LONDON • CAMBRIDGE • NEW YORK • SHARJAH

Copyright © Tom Walton 2023

The right of Tom Walton to be identified as author of this work has been asserted by the author in accordance with sections 77 and 78 of the Copyright, Designs and Patents Act 1988.

All rights reserved. No part of this publication may be reproduced, stored in a retrieval system, or transmitted in any form or by any means, electronic, mechanical, photocopying, recording, or otherwise, without the prior permission of the publishers.

Any person who commits any unauthorised act in relation to this publication may be liable to criminal prosecution and civil claims for damages.

This is a work of fiction. Names, characters, businesses, places, events, locales, and incidents are either the products of the author's imagination or used in a fictitious manner. Any resemblance to actual persons, living or dead, or actual events is purely coincidental.

A CIP catalogue record for this title is available from the British Library.

ISBN 9781035833993 (Paperback)
ISBN 9781035834006 (ePub e-book)

www.austinmacauley.com

First Published 2023
Austin Macauley Publishers Ltd®
1 Canada Square
Canary Wharf
London
E14 5AA

Chapter 1: All Things Bright and Beautiful

"Ow much is a pint of cider?"

Chris looked distastefully at the greasy-haired youth studying a handful of small change leaning against the bar. The youth drew heavily on a cigarette and attempted to blow smoke rings "I said ow much is a pint of cider."

Chris put down the glass he had been drying for the past 10 minutes. "Three pounds twenty, the same as it was last night."

"Ow much is half a cider?" A quick reckoning of his current financial situation appeared to dictate that a pint was probably out of the question. "One pound and sixty pence, anything else," came the reply as Chris returned to wiping the glass.

"I'll ava an arf," said the youth counting the handful of small change into neat piles on the immaculately polished bar. Chris pulled the half pint of cider, placed it on the bar and scooped up the handful of loose coins, and dropped them in the till without bothering to count them. "Ta, guvner," said the youth as he shuffled off towards the pool table where a couple of his mates were already seated.

Chris idly carried on polishing the glass and looking around the bar. It was by any standard immaculate in every detail, exposed wooden beams, highly polished horse brasses, a little tacky perhaps but Chris liked them, so they stayed, a small aquarium of brightly coloured tropical fish. This was it, the culmination of Chris's dreams. This picturesque little pub, nestling on a hillside overlooking a quiet seaside cove was all Chris had dreamt of working for years as a senior management consultant.

Life was indeed perfect, made especially so when his boring and nagging wife of 13 years decided that Chris's dream was not for her and promptly up and left him for a used car salesman to live in Spain. With no kids to worry about, the divorce was easy leaving him to swiftly replace her in the matrimonial bed, maybe too swiftly, with Shirly, a shapely local barmaid who had all the physical attributes of a saucy postcard and an imaginative wet dream rolled perfectly into one. As far as Chris was concerned, she ticked all the boxes.

If only the customers were a more select bunch.

Chris looked at the small group of locals sitting in their usual spots at the other end of the bar. Usual faces in usual seats, almost akin to ancestral seats to which anyone else having the temerity to sit were quickly made to feel uncomfortable enough to move on.

The usual two sat in their seats, saying little other than to request more beer.

Richard, a 67-year-old retired engineer and lifelong pessimist, who hated everyone and everything. Any subject matter would be met with a pessimistic or sarcastic response without a moment's thought. Beside him was his brother Ted, an amiable enough thin-faced chap who said little and spent even less.

Today they were joined by Mark, a 58-year-old bespectacled pint hugger dressed in his usual off-white threadbare collared shirt and shapeless baggy kneed trousers, with a shiny behind. He knew, or thought he knew everything and everything on any given subject. The fact of the matter was that if he read anything he'd stop as soon as he thought he had all the salient points and make up the rest. This often meant he came to the wrong conclusion on any matter he chose to give his opinion on, whether asked for it or not. Prone to over-exaggeration and overstating, his part in life's grand scheme was usually best ignored, which is what Richard did at the best of times unless of course there was some mileage in mercilessly making him the butt of the joke.

To be honest, Richard hated Mark.

Ted downed the last of his pint and placed the empty glass on the bar pushing it slightly towards Richard, hoping that a free refill was on its way. "Fuck off, it's your shout," Richard said pointedly to Ted without taking his eyes off the calendar he had been staring at for the past 10 minutes. Now turning his attention to Mark, he said, "So where are you working now since getting the push from your last place?" He really didn't want a reply, but hopefully, Mark's reply would give him something to latch on to as a good source of ridicule.

Ted was still managing to avoid buying a round.

Mark shifted his stance slightly. Holding his half-empty glass to his right shoulder with the other hand pulled up the tatty shapeless trousers, the waistband curling over the tatty brown belt that was holding them up. "Since the unpleasantness at my last employment that left me with no other option except resign my position, I have embarked on another career path, one that combines the fight against unlawfulness with the understated relationship between man and his best friend in the animal kingdom joining forces to combat the growing tide of wanton illegal acts and safeguard the future of and property of all law-abiding citizens, furthermore I…"

Richard seized the opportunity.

"Oh, so you're a fucking security guard, man and his best friend, bollocks, where the fuck do you keep this four-legged crime fighter anyway?"

Things in the bar were taking the usual downhill trajectory, which Chris ignored for now.

Mark looked a little hurt by Richard's crude comments belittling his new career, sniffed, pushed his glasses back up his nose and took a sip of his warm beer. "In my new position, I am officially referred to as a Level 1 mobile security operative with canine response capabilities and as a matter of fact, the canine response, as we in the security industry prefer to call it, is outside of the garden; he likes the company of small children."

"I don't give a rat arse what you call it, I hate all animals, cats, dogs, rabbits, goldfish, the bloody lot," muttered Richard. "Bloody dogs shouldn't be allowed in pubs, great hairy bags of shit, the lot of them," Richard retorted happy in the knowledge that he had dealt a blow to his pet hate.

Mark's comment that the dog was in the garden made Chris look out of the window where indeed the furry saviour of East Sussex was. A grimace spread across his face, "Mark, go and get that bloody dog out of my beer garden; it's lying on its side licking its balls, it's putting people off their beer."

Sure enough, the large brown elderly dog of indeterminate pedigree was lost in a world of self-gratification, making sloppy munching noises as it lapped, licked and gobbled intently at its pooch pleaser, much to the disgust of several patrons enjoying their meal in a basket.

Ted again nudged his empty glass a little more towards Richard. Mark put his glass down and headed to the beer garden to put an end to the dog's intense self-molestation.

"Bet you wish you could do that," said Ted, as Chris, tired of waiting for one of them to ask for another drink, poured a fresh pint into Ted's glass.

"Do what?" He replied.

"What that dog is doing right now," said Ted nodding towards the door that led to the beer garden.

Snatching a glance out of the window, Chris replied, "Well, actually I wouldn't mind."

"What? You mean you'd give yourself a nosh if you could reach that far," said Ted in an incredulous tone looking at Chris in disbelief.

"No, you said what the dog is doing right now, and right now he's got his face halfway up that French bird's skirt, six-forty please." Chris placed the second refilled glass on the bar. As Richard showed no sign of paying for the drinks, Ted handed over a £10 note.

Taking a sip from his fresh pint, Richard looked around the bar, "Where's the East Sussex bullshitter got too?" Chris looked out of the window into the garden.

"Well, it appears the unique and underestimated relationship that exists between man and dog has gone tits up, the dog's got his leg in its mouth and is dragging him around the garden."

Richard and Ted hurried to the window to join Chris and watch Mark try and free his leg from the dog's mouth. The harder he pulled, the harder the dog bit down; the more Mark howled, the dog got excited further. Customers were now moving rapidly away from the affray in what seemed certain to be a kill and akin more to scenes from a David Attenborough Serengeti documentary, than a beer garden in East Sussex. Nothing short of shooting the dog dead seemed to be the only solution to Mark's predicament.

"Fiver says the fucker chews it off and eats it before help arrives," said Richard, enjoying the spectacle far more than was appropriate.

"What help?" Ted said and returned to sipping his pint.

"Has someone called for help?" Chris said.

Chapter 2: Happy Trails – The Great Outdoors

A short downhill walk from the pub was Happy Trails, a camping and caravanners dream. Twelve acres of well-laid out, serviced caravan pitches and acres of flat grass, ideal for tents. Row upon row of neatly defined pitches, well-kept lawns and the odd flower bed scattered here and there. A reasonably well-stocked fishing lake added to its popularity for the young and old. With spotless facilities and a small on-site shop that sold all the basics at far from basic prices made it a popular venue with campers of all ages.

All this was owned and managed by Dan O'Connor and his wife Tina, a middle-aged couple from deepest Lincolnshire whose story was that they were seeking fresh opportunities when they bought the place, and not running from a family of crazed travellers that Dan had sold some dodgy caravans which had ultimately led to several of the family doing time with Her Majesty.

Dan spent most of his day in his office behind the main reception, attempting to beat the world smoking record while studying local supermarket whisky offers, while his wife of 10 years toiled away in the office dealing with the day-to-day administration of a busy site. They were an unlikely couple,

Dan, nine years Tina's senior, had struck gold when he chanced upon Tina's profile on the 'Desperate but Hopeful' dating site for broadminded adults.

It read.

"Bubbly dark-haired, vivacious, 25, just out of a long-term relationship, 40-24-32, fit energetic, enthusiastic, fun-loving, outdoors type, looking for a man to have fun times, long walks, intimate meals and future happiness." Dan recalled kissing the page and muttering, "Fucking bingo, big tits, on the rebound, looking for serious adventurous knobbing, just the girl for me," as he hurriedly pulled on a pair of reasonably unsoiled pants before sitting down at his laptop to compose a suitable reply.

He responded.

"Hi, Tina, I'm Dan, outgoing, young at heart, fit, sensitive, perhaps too sensitive when it comes to matters of the heart; I love the outdoors, long walks, and intimate meals. I volunteer at a local animal shelter and a halfway house for young adults, as I passionately believe young people need a guiding hand to get them on their feet (the latter he actually did on the odd occasion as it usually meant a steady stream of fit young birds who'd do anything for a couple of cans of White Lightening super strength cider). It's just my way of giving something back, I hope we can meet and explore our common interests, who knows where it could lead?"

If that doesn't get her gagging for it and dropping her pants fuck all will, thought Dan as he pressed the send button and scratched his balls.

After several successful dates where Dan had laid on the romantic charm, excusing the knackered caravan he was living in, as wanting to get closer to nature and the smell of cheap aftershave masking his adversity to soap and water, Tina was smitten, or perhaps permanently pissed as all they appeared to have in common was drink to excess and shag. Tina was now a permanent fixture in Dan's life and had moved into the squalid caravan, now referring to it lovingly as their 'home.'

Since moving in, she had totally cleaned the place from top to bottom, washing piles of used, re-used and re-re-used again clothes, which in fairness made the place smell a bit better than it did. Several black bin liners of fag ends were removed and the old gold interior she thought she had started cleaning turned out to be nicotine staining due to the chain-smoking Dan did all day with the windows closed. Nice little pictures, small vases of fake flowers and plastic animal sculptures now decorated the shelves as opposed to old underpants and socks that were kicked off in drunken attempts at undressing.

All was now sweetness and light.

Tina loved her new life; well, she would love anything because Dan was her last throw of the romantic dice as all she had to show for her 42 years on this planet, was the clothes she stood up in. As far as she was concerned, she'd bagged the man of her dreams; he had little expectation in life, no ambition and if he had a few quid in his pocket for fags and booze and the occasional sordid little dalliance or sexting, he wanted for nothing else. Sure, he came from good stock, a little bit of old money but that had all run dry for him when his parents disowned him and cut him off from any future access to their money.

The money to buy the site came from the only successful deal he had ever done, although the taxman was trying to track

Dan down for his share. At 53, shortish, beer-bellied and bald, missing a front tooth that he'd knocked out collapsing in a drunken stupor, for him, Tina was the ideal woman. Easily led, easily convinced that whatever 'her man' said was the truth, a self-made dog's body that Dan regularly took advantage of. Why wouldn't he? A few months after they met, he would occasionally throw in tempting visions of a future married life together to keep her quiet and hopeful. "As soon as my accountant gets the taxman off my back and gets me the half million, they owe me, the sooner we can get married," was a favourite ploy and one that Tina believed whole heartedly.

She honestly believed that there was a secret stash of cash tucked away for a rainy day, the fact is it could be monsoonal and there wouldn't be a single penny forthcoming wasn't something she was prepared to listen to. Her man had told her, so it must be real.

Tina's heart had leapt at his marriage proposal, which just happened to coincide with rumours of Dan's indiscretions with a local woman. Although she'd hardly be a blushing bride, after all, she'd been around the block a few times, but she'd scrub up enough to make a decent fist of it.

Her biggest problem was that Dan's inherent laziness left him with too much time on his hands and as the saying goes *the devil finds work for idle hands*, if he does, he'd found the ideal disciple in Dan. At 53 with his 'best' years behind him, Dan still liked to think that he had something to offer the opposite sex, even if it was the odd photo of his penis in various stages of arousal according to how much alcohol he had consumed which made the gallery of his cock depict anything resembling the Hunchback of Notre Dame to

Nelsons Column, which he would share with any woman who asked or didn't ask as he was still going to send it anyway. Sexting was, as far as Dan was concerned better than any wank mag and he was an avid reader of dubious publications, the more salacious the title, the better.

Although Tina was aware of Dan's love of the genital selfie, as with most things, Dan managed to convince her that it was just a phase.

Dan was a people person, if 'the people' in question were rich, he was a closet snob, or gullible, so he could fleece them out of whatever he could get.

Tina was the complete opposite. She saw the good in the worst of people and would fall for any cock and bull hard luck story, after all, she was with Dan!

Together they made a good pair.

She was deaf and blind to his transgressions, and he didn't give a fuck if there was a clean caravan, clean(ish) ironed clothes, as Tina was every bit as much a chain smoker as Dan the clothes already came with a pre-lived-in odour, and sex on demand, he was a happy man.

The site was as good as any on the South Coast and provided an above-average income with little outgoings. Being mainly a cash business, it afforded a tax-free income if the taxman didn't catch up with them. Open all year round, the steady stream of cash kept rolling in and with only four members of staff, Aaron and Tristan, who Dan thought were a couple of gays but hadn't confirmed as such, and Bob and Maud, who were employed at the site when Dan bought it and had their own caravan that Maud kept in spotless condition.

As all four members of staff would work for less than minimum wage Dan would remind them daily of their mission in life. "I pay you to do all things I can't be bothered to do when that doesn't suit you any longer, you know where the gate is." In some ways, it was as good a mission statement as any. In all it looked likely that their standard of living would continue unabated for the near future, with half a dozen permanent residents Dan could be assured there was always a demand for his over-priced shop essentials.

This weekend saw the long summer bank holiday and the site was fully booked, although Dan would always find room for the odd extra caravan or tent should they offer to pay extra, or in whisky/cider or wine, didn't matter which, if there was lots of it and the latecomers were eternally grateful.

First among the arrivals was Dave and Carol Quinn. New to caravanning, Dave had been one of the lucky ones to have a decent win on the National Lottery and had splashed out on a new Land Rover Discovery and the latest four-berth caravan, the holiday weekend marked the embarkation of what they hoped would be the first of many long and happy caravanning adventures. Dave booked in at the office where Tina, Tristan and Aaron were waiting.

The usual exchange of cash was reciprocated with a handful of South Coast attraction leaflets and information on the camp rules and shop opening times. With the formalities over, Aaron jumped on his bicycle and led Dave and Carol to their pitch.

Returning to the office, he busied himself organising the local tourist hotspot leaflets and waited for the rush.

Chapter 3: Animal Cruelty

Meanwhile, back in the beer garden at The Seagull, Mark bravely battled on. "Kick the bastard in the head," pleaded Mark to a group of customers as the dog dragged him past their table. The battle continued to gain in ferocity and the more the dog exerted itself, a bout of overwhelming flatulence erupted. The greater the exertion, the worse the smell emitting from its bowels became.

The patrons that were going to exit from the affray were by now transfixed on the battle of good versus evil playing out before them; more than half were rooting for the dog to win.

Mark kicked out vainly at the dog's head with his free leg. A foul stench invaded his nostrils invoking severe gagging, "It's shit itself, its shit itself, for fucks sake, someone shoot it," Mark wailed. The onlookers' eyes narrowed at the use of such expletives and their desire for the dog to win intensified, but they couldn't help but agree that the smells coming from the dog were disgusting. "It's fucking eating me alive, kill it, kill it, for fucks sake, kill it." That just about sealed his fate, if any of the onlookers felt any pity at all for him, they certainly didn't now.

"You ought to stop antagonising that poor dog and take your leg out of its mouth," said a bleached blonde mother of two as she shielded her offspring's eyes from the ensuing carnage. "You ought to be bloody well ashamed of yourself," she continued while kicking spitefully at Mark's fingers as he grimly held onto the leg of her table trying to extricate himself from the foul-smelling beast.

The beast, now bored with this game relaxed; its vice-like grip on Mark's leg just long enough for him to roll into a foetal position with his arms across his head. His shapeless trousers, now covered in dog slobber, he lay motionless. If he stayed completely still, perhaps the dog would think he was dead, which wasn't far from the truth. The beast lay motionless staring at Mark just waiting for him to move, watching, watching, waiting and occasionally moving and inching closer. The dog's slobbered leg grew cold, but still gave off a strange odour, dog food mixed with chuff licking, unusually disgusting but in keeping with the beast's overall array of putrid smells.

Chris, Ted, and Richard, now bored with Mark's lack of conviction to free himself gave up watching what was now an inevitable lost cause and went back to what they were doing.

Chris cleared the table in the front garden and looked down at the caravan site to see how busy it was.

Although modest spenders in general, the site did add a bit extra to trade during the summer months and they were always welcome as a diversion from his usual clientele.

Better get Shirly to wear the low-cut plunging neckline top. If it offended the female trade, it certainly kept their menfolk coming back for another eyeful and if that didn't work, it pressed the right buttons for him.

Chapter 4: Howdy Doody Yoody

At the reception, things were getting busy. A steady stream of punters was arriving at the site. Tina as always had a smile on her face and a fag in her mouth. Dan, as usual, was missing. Probably back in the caravan smoking or scanning the lonely-hearts websites to select the next recipient of his personal dick pics.

Tina fearing the worst decided to look for him on the pretence of needing his help, and he was the one needing help. As she crossed the driveway, a huge American camper swung through the gates. Pulling up into an available parking space, the door flew open, and a mountain of a man exited, stretching in the warm sunshine, displaying his muscular physique. It was enough to make Tina take a second glance.

Chuck and Debbie DiAngelo were taking their first break in their newly shipped-in Winnebago. Chuck, 6'6", United States Marine Corps Master Sergeant, with enough pearly white teeth, could be mistaken for a great white shark, strolled purposefully into reception. Standing in the doorway, his imposing physique blocked out the sunlight making Tristan look up from the pocket mirror he was using to dab ointment on his puss-filled acne spots. On seeing Chuck, he swiftly brushed to bloody puss-stained tissue under the table.

"Hey there, fella, we're booked to stay a couple of nights, do we check in here?" Chuck's eyes took a minute or so to get used to the dim lighting in the office but soon were focussing on Tristan's thin pale oozing face which had bits of tissue stuck to the more persistent bleeders.

"Sure is," said Tristan in a put-on American accent that immediately annoyed Chuck. Tristan sat at the computer and tapped away bringing up the booking. "Just the two nights, is it?" Tristan said like a Blackpool landlady.

"Guess so," replied Chuck trying not to get too close to Tristan's face and wondering if leprosy had been eradicated in the UK.

"How big is it?" Tristan asked.

"Big is what?" Chuck looked puzzled.

"That?" Tristan said jabbing a pencil at the window where the camper was parked outside.

"Oh that, fourteen metres, why?"

"We charge by the metre," Tristan responded studying a ready reckoner taped to the desk. "Fourteen, fourteen," said Tristan running his pencil up and down the chart. "No, can't do fourteen, it'll have to be fifteen," said Tristan looking up at the full extent of Chuck's stature and standing back a little intimidated at the man mountain.

"Why?" Chuck loomed a little closer, but far enough away to avoid any outfall should Tristan's infected face explode.

Swallowing nervously and trying in vain to conceal his fear Tristan replied, "We charge by the metre and our list goes from 6 to 10 metres then 12 and then 15 metres." Chuck puffed out his chest, breathing in exaggeratingly through his nose like an angry bull.

"Why fifteen?"

Tristan pointed feebly at the ready reckoner, "Well, we charge from…"

Chuck held up a huge hand that could have swallowed all of Tristan's head cutting Tristan off mid-flow, "Don't you go repeating yourself, boy, I can see I ain't going to git no sense outta ya," Chuck said pulling his wallet from the back pocket of his impressively tight faded blue jeans and curtly tossing his Amex card on the counter.

"Do me a favour, boy and use one of those Kleenex when you pick that up," Chuck said in an authoritative manner making the request more like a command and pointing a huge finger to a super-sized box of tissues.

"Why?" Tristan asked, looking a little confused.

"Cos I don't wanna get your pus all over it," Chuck looked menacing.

"Shithouse," muttered Tristan under his breath. He couldn't stand Americans, all white teeth, clean hair, and healthy living, or at least the ones that he had met which up until now was just Chuck. Tristan followed Chuck's command and picked up the card with a tissue. "Kleenex, Kleenex, what the fuck is that about," Tristan muttered quietly.

"Everything ok, honey?" Through the door walked Debbie, Chuck's wife, diminutive in stature with breasts far too big for one so slender and flowing locks of wavy pure blonde hair, immaculate makeup, and pure white perfect teeth. Her perfume filled the air as much as her tits filled the tight t-shirt emblazoned with the Stars and Stripes and just short enough to reveal a perfectly flat-tanned midriff. She wiggled a little closer to Chuck nuzzling into him.

"Sure, sweetlips, me and the boy here are just tying up the paperwork." He patted Debbie's bum through her tight faded blue Levi's.

With almost perfect timing, Dan breezed into the office inhaling in the sweet perfume and fixing his gaze upon this stunning creature. Like a guided missile, Dan had homed in on the tiny temptress the moment she exited the camper van.

"Good morning, I hope my staff is looking after you this morning." The bullshit mode was turned up to maximum. Dan couldn't tear his eyes off those fantastic tits or that perfectly rounded bum and leant closer to the counter hoping to hide the lazy lob that was growing in his trousers.

"Well," said Chuck, "there is one thing that confuses me, this charging thing, no fourteen-metre rate?" Dan looked at the ready reckoner and then disapprovingly at Tristan.

"Come, come, Tristan, it's not every day we have our friends from across the pond visit us, I'm sure we can do better than that," and immediately dropped the rate ludicrously.

"How about the ten-metre rate?" At this kind gesture, Chuck shrugged and nodded his head in approval.

"Gee, honey, ain't that kind?" Debbie giggled, adding fuel to Dan's burgeoning problem. Chuck thought it saved him $40 and since arriving in the UK, he couldn't understand how a shitty little island where it rained all the time could be so expensive.

"Tristan, can you do the honours for our friends and put them in the resident's area, it's so much quieter there?" It was the perfect perving distance from Dan's shabby dwelling.

Dan turned to Chuck and Debbie, now on the verge of exploding. "Can I invite you to a little get-together we have here occasionally, nothing too flashy, just a few beers with a barbeque, we, my wife, Tina and I (trying to give an air of respectability to it) like to invite a few residents and visitors; it's a bit like being invited to the captain's table on board ship, tomorrow middayish?" Dan quipped smiling through the missing front tooth where his denture should be.

Utter bollocks thought Tristan running Chuck's card through the payment machine. As Chuck was now occupied in conversation with Dan and he was no longer the focus of Chuck's attention, Tristan scratched his balls with Chuck's card and ran it across a couple of the juicier spots on his face before placing it back on the counter. Take that, Howdy Doodie Yoody!

Tristan and Aaron were more than familiar with Dan's get-togethers. They were always a shit show of monumental proportions and they always ended badly. On the bright side, there was always plenty of free food and booze and on the plus side, Dan refused to eat any of the sub-standard crap he sold in the site shop, so a bit of a decent feed was always welcome. Although he could never be described as a paragon of healthy eating even, he had to draw the line somewhere. The trick to getting the best out of Dan's get-togethers was to pick the right moment between Dan's inebriated innuendo and drunken crudity to make one's excuses and leave.

Chuck now finished talking to Dan and accepting his kind gesture of a reduced rate and the invite to the Saturday gathering turned back to the counter and picked up his card placing it in his mouth while fumbling for his wallet from his back pocket. Debbie helped herself to some of the tourist information sheets which presented Dan with an opportunity to strike up conversation. "Looking for anything particular?"

Dan hoped she would say getting him to shag the living daylights out of her, but her desire for local history brought him back to Earth with a bump, disappointed at her unimaginative reply.

Chuck fired up the camper while Debbie climbed the steps turning to smile at Dan.

He was certain that she was wiggling her bum at him and as far as he was concerned, getting in her pants was definite. As the camper slowly moved off, Dan gave a little wave, "See you later."

This could be the best holiday weekend ever.

Chapter 5: The Great Outdoors

Now neatly set up on the pitch and eager to open some of the new equipment he'd bought especially for the weekend, Dave Quinn unpacked a brand-new barbeque from the back of the Land Rover. It was a present from his wife Carol to mark their foray into caravanning. As most men do, Dave felt that barbequing and cooking meat in the open air was primaeval and something men were born to do. Playing with fire was instinctive and brought out the hunter-gatherer and a man should dress as such. Far from donning animal skins, all Dave could find was an off-white pair of shorts left over from his footballing days in the Wapping Sunday League. It was a bit of a squeeze but with a bit of adjustment to the family jewels they were on, like a second skin drawn taught across his lower body.

Feeling a little self-conscious of his skinny ghostly white torso exposed to the elements and shoeless, real men don't wear shoes when cooking, Dave placed the box on the ground and began arranging the various parts neatly in order. He looked admiringly at the shiny new barbeque. Made and Designed in Birmingham, it said on the box. Dave pondered momentarily the vast engineering tradition the midlands had. "Bloody quality, true engineering craftsmanship," he said to himself as he looked around to see if anyone was watching him before getting into the assembly phase.

The barbeque far from being manufactured by engineers in Birmingham was thrown together in Russia and made of remodelled parts meant for the now defunct nuclear programme, swiftly abandoned after the unfortunate events in Chernobyl. Cobbled together in the backstreets of Leningrad by out-of-work scientists who had engineered the biggest nuclear balls up the world had ever seen and shipped in plain boxes across the unsuspecting planet ready for any get-rich-quick merchant to slap their own labels on.

As Dave studied the instructions, Carol busied herself preparing the food. Of course, there were burgers, Meetee Ranch Style 100% Meat, proclaimed the packet, which in Layman's terms meant they consisted of little more than lips, bums, and testicles of a variety of factory-farmed animals ground to a pulp with as enough cereal and flavourings to bind it together and hide the putrid taste just long enough for them to cook. To accompany this, Carol laid out a dozen chicken legs which the packet described as 'Free Range' Loosely interpreted as old broilers that were past cracking out an egg every hour and had spent so much time in artificial light, they saw slaughter as a merciful release. "There," said Carol tilting her head to one side, admiring the way in which the pending feast was laid out.

Outside kneeling on the grass and now bathed in warm sunlight, Dave squinted at the instructions eager to get the build finished and the cooking underway.

1. Peeces lay out
2. Skudrivver peeces holes wit skrues in fitting number

3. Kept away from materells of flames
4. Fill fuool hole diesel burn lumpy
5. Strikt mitch and litten fuool
6. Hot to weight and food adinkt7

Dave worked feverishly interpreting the vague instructions as he went until there before him glowing in the warm mid-morning sunshine stood his new Outdoorsman 2000 Bar-Be-Q. All was now ready. Hands trembling with anticipation, Dave added the free charcoal that came with the set and for good measure a little extra lighter fluid and struck a match immediately igniting the fuel.

As the flames took hold, tiny wisps of thick acrid smoke began to rise which became thicker and acrider, the hotter the fire became and began drifting across the campsite and hanging ominously in the air. "Never mind. It's just paint burning off, it'll die down in a minute."

If only.

As the heat increased at an alarming rate, smoke belched from the now red-hot molten mass and started to drift ominously across the site.

"You're an ignorant prick, put it out," someone shouted in the near distance. Camping camaraderie was being tested to breaking point.

Another 10 minutes passed and the catastrophic consequences of Dave's once-prized barbeque were becoming all too evident. The situation was getting worse and if he could have seen them through the apocalyptic smoke, Dave would have been aware of the looks of sheer hate directed toward him.

The first signs of panic were appearing on Dave's face. Birds were now dropping out of the sky like feathered confetti at which point anyone with a shred of common sense would have admitted defeat and called in the professionals.

Carol looked on in horror from the safety of their new caravan as Dave fought manfully to control the belching mass from spewing more noxious ash and smoke heavenwards. As Seagulls and pigeons continued to fall, the colour began to drain from Dave's face, not that anyone would notice as his pale features were now a sooty black.

Dave's mind raced, what could have gone wrong?

Instructions, where's the bloody instructions, there must be a fault-finding paragraph in there somewhere.

Wading through the blackened and sooty remnants of what was once a thriving colony of Gannets Dave grabbed at the instructions and through reddened, bloodshot, and profusely watering eyes began to read out loud.

"Put that out, you ignorant shite." Things were turning ugly with Dave's fellow campers. If only I could, winced Dave.

Campers downwind of the debacle were now in survival mode and taking shelter. The Lincs and Notts Over 70s Camping Club that met every summer holiday weekend huddled together in their huge function tent and began to sing songs from the war, if Vera Lynn worked against the Hun it'd work against some eco-terrorist.

Chapter 6: Good Subject Matter

Mark lay on the ground, still convinced that any movement would see a return of hostilities and unaware that the beast was now being fed scraps of a chicken in the basket pub lunch.

Inside sitting quietly in the corner sat Paul, late 60s, skinny, with long grey hair, thin bearded, aged hippy type, with tie-dyed t-shirt, elephant pants, and sandals. Resident at Happy Trails for a good number of years, Paul was a frequent visitor to the pub. No one was sure what Paul did in his past working life, there was some talk of him being a foreign correspondent for a broadsheet paper in Fleet Street as he sometimes referred to his extensive foreign travel and a liking for dark-skinned girls. It was speculation and a good subject matter for the Saturday gatherings.

Paul was well-read, he was never without a book tucked under his arm but had an annoying habit of claiming he knew the author, "Oh so-and-so, yes he's a good friend of mine, sent me this pre-production copy to look over." The fact that some of the authors had died years before Paul was born didn't seem to bother him, after all, why let the truth spoil a good yarn!

Paul had an air about him, although a bit on the scruffy side he gave an educated, learned, intellectual impression that made people regard him as someone to engage with. The truth of the matter was that Paul was a conspiracy theorist and in his often alcohol fuelled state any tiny thing could spark the most wild and outlandish conspiracy. Paul downed the last of his beer and placed the empty glass on the bar. Richard looked at him "OK, cat weasel," Richard had chanced on fresh game to ridicule.

Paul ignored him, as Paul would often refer to Richard as, 'That detestable man of little intelligence.' Chris refilled the glass and placed it on the bar, turning to Richard, "Enough, it's going to be a long day and I can do without your constant harassment of my customers."

Richard shrugged, "I was only asking after cat weasels health."

"I said enough, if you can't be civil, then go and drink elsewhere," Chris said knowing that the next pub was three miles away. This sudden rebuke made Richard pick up his glass and move to a table in the front garden.

Thanking Chris, Paul took up his seat again and started to read his latest book making sure that the title was clearly visible to everyone. It was uncommon for someone, that didn't know him, to ask 'Good book or unusual title?' This gave Paul the chance to strike up an unwanted conversation which he would steer to whatever his latest conspiracy theory was. The moon landings were a favourite always bound to stir up conversation. Trying to convince people that he knew all the astronauts personally and that NASA had called on him for advice was a stretch too far.

A couple on a walking holiday sat at the next table and while the woman was using the facilities her partner did the usual. "Good book?"

Leaving his gaze on the page, Paul took a few seconds longer to respond, making it look like he had reached a crucial point in the text. "Yesss, it's very good, better than I expected actually." Paul raised his gaze and let the words hang in the air a bit to entice this chap in.

"Music is it, the book, music?" The guy nodded at the book, not knowing that the trap was all but sprung.

"Oh no, no, no," replied Paul leaning back in his chair with a smug chuckle and brushing his long grey hair back with his hands. "My friend, don't let the title mislead you, *the Song Lines* in the title aren't to do with music as you'd know it, it's Australian Aboriginal, I spent a considerable amount of time with a tribe in the NT back in the 70s, the tribe was the…" Paul continued to spit and croak an undistinguishable name that couldn't possibly be verified or repeated.

"How's that then, I mean how does music not be music as I'd know it?" The chap looked confused and had now been joined by the man's wife, making Paul's semi-captive audience swell by one.

Seeing the woman was about to go to the bar, Paul chugged his beer and placed the empty glass in the middle of his table, but in their direction.

"Can I get you one?" The woman asked.

"How kind," Paul feigned gratitude, "just a small scotch, the landlord knows which one."

She looked at the empty half-pint glass in front of Paul and back at Paul, a little confused and irritated at being taken advantage of she replied, "And the beer," thinking she'd shame him into changing his drink.

"Oh, if you insist, I find if drink scotch on its own, it goes down too bloody quickly," Paul didn't do shame.

33

The woman acknowledging defeat went to the bar to order the drinks leaving Paul with what he guessed was her husband. He continued, "The author, a great friend of mine sent me this book in gratitude for the huge input I had on his work, not many people can speak or understand the…" and he spat and croaked out another unrecognisable tribal name.

"Oh, I thought," the man tried to interject, but Paul didn't do interjection and not when he was just getting into his self-important stride and cut him off.

"You see as the aboriginal doesn't or at least didn't, have a universally recognised written language, communication, the written word you understand, was impossible." The woman returned from the bar and placed a small, but expensive, scotch and a half pint of beer in front of Paul. Without hesitating Paul downed the scotch shaking any excess into the beer. "Well, not until they were visited by beings from another planet and well, that changed everything." He looked for approval and admiration at his tale by raising his eyebrows and nodding in an all-knowing manner. He rubbed his finger around the inside of the now-empty whisky glass and sucked the residue off.

"You mean aliens, like Martians or something?" The man added before Paul again cut him off.

"Not Martians, definitely not Martians, no, far too far away, somewhere closer, like the moon." The couple stared at each other, how on Earth, to excuse the pun, did a relaxed coastal stroll and pub lunch turn into a lecture by a madman!" Before he could stop himself, the man added, "The moon, there isn't life on the moon," bollocks he thought, I've invited more of his fantasy. Another chance for Paul to slip in more fantastical nonsense, "Oh, isn't there, Buzz told me what he saw, only a few really know why the Yanks went there and what they saw, if I told you what Buzz told me."

The pair sat open-mouthed as Paul continued. "Mars, come on now, this isn't fantasy land, you are away with the fairies if you think there's life on Mars, well not the life that NASA is prepared to admit to yet but believe me when I tell you I've met the 'visitors' and none of them came from Mars, close but not Mars…"

Time to make an exit, the pair got to their feet, leaving their drinks, made an excuse that they were running late, and hurried to the door. "See you soon I hope, how about tonight, I'm always here." They disappeared through the door not caring to look back or further acknowledge Paul in any way in case it encouraged more lunacy.

Paul looked pleased with imparting his wisdom to a pair of strangers, even better their drinks were untouched. He slid their pint of lager and large white wine closer, that'll do for lunchtime.

Chris stared in disbelief at Paul's downright cheek. "I've got to do something about that bloody man scaring customers away with his stupid theories," he muttered.

Exiting into the beer garden, the couple fleeing from Paul's fantastical stories now came upon a huddled, dishevelled figure laying on the ground and largely ignored by the rest of the patrons.

"Bloody hell, what on Earth is happening here, why are they all ignoring him, he looks hurt?" The man said to his wife. Making another huge mistake, the couple helped Mark to his rather unsteady feet and immediately smelled Mark's dog-slobbered trousers. Dog chuff and Winalot made the man struggle for breath as his wife gagged profusely. "Are you ok?" He asked of an eternally grateful Mark who was now hanging onto the pair for support and refuge.

"Has it gone, the beast, has it gone?" Mark's wild eyes stared at them.

"Gone, beast, what beast?" The man replied staring back at Mark in alarm while his wife scanned the immediate surrounding for something evil. "The beast, has it gone, big brown beast, teeth, big teeth, smell like hell, biting gnawing beast," Mark made no sense. Fearing they had stumbled across some Black Cult member after undergoing some sordid ritual, they dropped Mark back where he previously laid. Falling like a sack of potatoes, Mark resumed huddling, whimpering in the foetal position.

"Quick, run for the gate, they're all bloody mad here," the man commanded his wife who didn't need to be asked twice.

They were last seen making their way hurriedly back along the path, probably never to be seen again.

Chapter 7: Target Practice

Rubbing his sore, streaming eyes, Dave continued to scan through the instructions. *Where did I go wrong*, Dave thought, all I did was build a bloody barbeque as the heat continued to rise and the smoke intensified alarmingly.

Nervous strains of '*We'll meet again, don't know where, don't know when,*' chorused shakily from inside the pensioners' rally tent.

Ignoring them, Dave forced himself to work on.

1. Peeces lay out; yes, thought Dave, I can't have got that wrong.
2. Skudriver peeces holes with skrues in order fiiting; whatever that meant, Dave was sure he'd done it.
3. Kept away from materials of flames; fuck the materials with flames, he winced.

Opening the window slightly from the safety of their caravan, Carol cried out to her beloved husband, "Be careful, darling, be careful."

"Fuck off, halfwit," bellowed Dave as sheer panic manifested itself upon him.

Dave had never considered wife battering before, but it was sure becoming a strong contender for his next course of action.

"Shut the fucking window, you stupid bitch," he commanded as tears streamed readily from his nearly half-closed, bloodshot eyes. His smoke-ridden face twisted in confused agony as a pall of noxious fumes and smoke headed for his new caravan.

Disaster or not Carol, a quick-tempered redhead from Essex wasn't going to stand for that kind of language from anyone and especially not from the man who years previously she'd given herself so willingly on the back seat of his Ford Escort and continued to endure his somewhat unusual sexual tendencies.

Throwing caution to the wind, Carol threw open the caravan window. Her venom-filled eyes fixed upon Dave. "And fuck you too, you bum-shagger, go the fuck up in smoke for all I care," she screeched.

"Fuck you too, dog breath," Dave retorted.

Fifteen years of wedded bliss had literally gone up in smoke in less than 10 minutes.

Dave struggled on.

1. Fill fuel hole diesel burn lumpy. Fill fuool hole diesel burn lumpy, he muttered over and over; maybe repeating the instruction would suddenly become clear. Just what the fuck does it mean? Dave tried running the instruction through his mind in a Brummie accent.

No, that didn't work either.

Something clicked inside his head, Fill fuool hole diesel burn lumpy, Dave was finally beginning to see the light, which was more than the downwind campers at Happy Trails could.

Dave had failed to recognise that in the backstreets of Leningrad, ex-nuclear programme chief engineer and off-late barbeque production manager comrade, Yuri had resorted to Estuarine parlance when dictating the instruction after watching an episode of East Enders during one of his many vodka breaks. Yuri had watched an episode where Dirty Den talked about torching the Queen Vic and saying, "These'll burn," referring to a bunch of screwed-up newspapers he had shoved into the pub's letterbox. Phonetically translating, the instructions through his vodka-ravaged brain, Yuri was pleased at the result, perfect English. He dreamt of meeting Her Majiksy ther Qwean and being able to impress her with his immaculate grasp of the English language and engaging her in long conversations about corgis, horses and lots of other domesticated animals he had eaten.

The rest of the production team, most of which hardly spoke Russian, let alone any other language looked up to Yuri as an inspiration, although many still suffered from flashbacks to that dreadful day when the reactor was going critical and Chief Engineer Yuri assuring them, 'it's nuthink, trust me.'

Forgetting the rest of the piss awful instructions and cursing himself for not realising sooner, Dave stood back from the melting mass of twisted metal and plastic that was still spewing black smoke and ash high into the atmosphere. With eyes darting back and forth across the site, Dave looked vainly for some spectacular miracle to happen. "Bollocks, bollocks, bollocks," Dave cursed as any inspiration or semblance of a plan eluded him. A sudden loud hissing noise coming from the barbeque snapped his attention back to the source of his troubles.

"What now, for fucks sake?" Dave whined, bending down and using his arm to shield his face from the inferno. Squinting intently Dave could see the charcoal had begun to hiss. Looking puzzled, Dave squinted harder to try and make some sense of what he was looking at. Why the fuck would charcoal hiss, surely the stuff is made from dried trees or something. Crouching ever lower, Dave circled the barbeque rising up and down as he went to get a better look. No, it was the charcoal that was hissing and what was worse it was getting even louder and more threatening.

Escape, save yourself, a voice in Dave's head commanded. For once, Dave relied on his instincts and ran towards his now sooty caravan.

With each stride, Dave's skin-tight shorts began to split inch by inch until his wedding tackle hung free of its fetters and flapped flaccidly from side to side, not that he had noticed as self-preservation was the only thing now on his mind.

Reaching the caravan, Dave yanked wildly at the door only to find that Carol who was still more than a little upset had locked him out. "Let me in, for fucks sake," he hollered at the top of his voice while snatching a glance over his shoulder at the hissing inferno just in time to catch the first of what would be many small explosions. A small but perfectly-formed mushroom cloud formed over the top of what was once a barbeque and a shock wave that all but knocked him off his feet pushed him forward towards his impending sanctuary.

Dave pleaded with Carol, "I'm serious you, bitch, open the fucking door or I'll kick it in." There wasn't any hope of that as Dave's shoeless feet could barely support him let alone do any real damage to the caravan door.

Dave felt closer to his maker than he had ever done before.

"Fuck off," snarled Carol. Wedded bliss had without a doubt taken a turn for the worse in this once harmonious marriage.

'There'll be blue birds overrrr...' the petrified pensioners sang in loose harmony from the safety of the rally tent.

Still tugging frantically at the door, Dave swung around straining to see where the singing was coming from worried that a band of angels were descending to take him home. He scanned what he could see of the heavens through bloke smoke and now almost fully-closed eyes.

Things were taking on an apocalyptic air.

"Carol, you stupid fat bitch, open this fucking door," Dave's rants had taken on a more purposeful tone that she just had to take notice of.

Carol's anger had now subsided into tears of hurt and remorse, which were largely fuelled by a large measure of Sweet Martini that Dave had bought for their first night in their new caravan knowing that Carol had little resistance to it and usually pulled a few strokes when she had consumed half a bottle and remembered little of the sordid evening the next morning.

Flinging the door open, Carol sobbed, "Dave, I love you, Dave," which appeared to be the automatic response she had built up under the influence of Martini and having to endure his somewhat unethical and unnatural approach to sex between a married couple.

"Go fuck yourself," Dave responded harshly as he pushed past the now half-naked and remorseful Carol, who half-stoned on Martini and had automatically started to get her kit off.

"But Dave, I love you," wailed Carol.

"Not the fuck anymore, you don't," Dave hissed as he grabbed a towel and tried to wipe the tears and soot from his eyes.

Staggering backwards with her more than ample breasts swinging freely, Carol grabbed at Dave to steady herself in her drunken stupor sending the pair of them crashing onto the unmade bed. Dave landed on top with his face buried firmly in Carol's ample heaving cleavage.

What the fuck was happening, Dave's mind raced to make sense of the situation. One thing he did know was that now wasn't the time to play 'hide Timmy up the poopy tunnel.' Struggling for breath, Dave tried pulling himself free as the semi-comatose and over-hysterical Carol clung on.

Chapter 8: The War Spirit

Outside the rally tent, the apocalypse continued.

'Pack up your troubles in your old kit bag and smile, smile, smile...' Things by now were also beginning to deteriorate in the pensioners' tent. The hurried shelter sought by them to escape the developing catastrophic events outside the dimness of the tent had resulted in some unhappy pairings. Frank O'Leary a onetime merchant seaman, retired undertaker and lay preacher from Dublin found himself squeezed up close to Gloria Cummings, a 70-ish widowed 'Hooker Made Good' who portrayed herself to the other members of the group as a retired social secretary. At least some of her pretence was true as in her time she'd dressed up as all sorts of things, nurse, schoolgirl, deep sea diver, in fact, anything the punter was willing to pay for and the secretary had figured amongst them, several times in fact.

With all the confusion and the heady smell of canvas mingled with 4711 perfume and piss emanating from Gloria Watts's incontinence pad, Frank was beginning to feel an unfamiliar stirring in his loins. Although older by 50 plus years, Frank had 'known' Gloria once or twice when his ship was in Liverpool undergoing repairs. Those post-war years for a young sailor were a good life made better by a run ashore into the seedier venues around the ports where anything was freely available.

In those days, not everyone was enjoying the fruits of post-war England and a girl made a living where she could. Gusty Gloria, the Human Hurricane, as she had been nicknamed among the seafaring community had one peculiar 'trick' that kept the punters coming back.

She could drop her pants and could muster up enough force in her fanny to blow out a candle from five feet or eject a ping pong ball across the room. Tricks she would willingly perform for a shilling a go. There was no shortage of takers.

Engineering himself a little closer to Gloria Frank could feel her 46 D cup pushing provocatively into his side. "Gloria, Gloria," he whispered as her heaving bosoms continue to awaken his lustful, wicked urges, "Blow out the candle, Gloria," he muttered forgetting himself and rubbing up against her leg like a spaniel on heat.

In the semi-darkness of the tent, Gloria who was used to having men rub up against her had until now not paid much attention to Frank who she now gazed at in horror. Frank was now completely lost in pornographic reminiscences and judging by the bulge in his shorts close to the gravy stroke. "Shut up," she hissed into his ear which startled Frank back to his senses. Staring into her eyes, all Frank could do was blurt out, "Gusty, it's you."

In one awful moment, her dirty little secret and Frank's long-forgotten memories were brought back to the surface.

If she was going to maintain her air of respectability as a retiree and keep her shady past a secret, she had to think quickly. While Frank, still not believing he'd found the object of his youthful desires, turned to Gloria, "It's me, Frank, don't you remember, King George Tavern, Liverpool, 1958, surely you remember, the candle trick, can you still do it?"

It was do or die as far as Gloria was concerned. Grabbing Frank by the most intimate parts, she squeezed as hard as she could to shut Frank the fuck up.

"Gloriaaaaa," Frank moaned, "I knew you hadn't forgotten me." As Frank went further into sexual raptures, Gloria's dilemma deepened. "Oh, fuck," hissed Gloria and squeezed Frank's manhood harder. The harder she squeezed, the more Frank moaned in wanton pleasure and even though Frank was the impending undoing of her 'good' reputation, Gloria couldn't help being impressed by the size and response of Frank's manhood. Strange, she thought, it was not that long ago that I would have welcomed a bit of this.

By now, others in the tent had begun to stop singing and were taking an interest in Frank and Gloria.

"Gloria, Gloria," Frank moaned. Before he could start muttering anymore about the candle trick, Gloria pushed her ample bosom into Frank's face. "Oh fuck, I'm coming again," moaned Frank through her 46D cup. "There, there, dear," soothed Gloria stroking the back of Frank's hair and pushing his face even harder into her bosom and hoping that suffocation by mammary glands was not a capital offence. Bending a little closer to Frank's ear she hissed through clenched dentures, "Shut the fuck up, reverend, or you'll see the second coming quicker than most."

The thought of meeting his maker a good deal earlier than expected and without the opportunity to have confessed all, and today would take some confessing, seemed to jerk Frank back to his senses. Pulling his head free from Gloria's bosom, Frank gasped in fresh, well freshish, air. Tempted to re-bury his head into Gloria's gorgeous cleavage, Frank somehow knew that a repeat performance of the candle trick was out of the question.

Their fellow campers were beginning to see Frank and Gloria in a different light, a light that hadn't shone upon their lustless lives for a good number of years.

Singing had all but stopped but Beryl Watts insisted on one last chorus of 'Roll out the barrel,' if nothing else; the smell of strong cough sweets should be enough to stifle the musty aroma from numerous incontinence pads.

"Sing up everyone," she enthused.

"Fuck off," came the collective reply.

Frank and Gloria, no longer the main attraction continued to hiss harsh words at each other while the closed tent flaps diminished the oxygen supply considerably rendering most of the occupants a little sleepy and ready for a nap.

Outside, another small explosion from the melting barbeque refocussed the ones still awake on the impending doom and meeting their maker.

Chapter 9: The Festival Season

Sleeping blissfully unaware of the commotion, Andy Gouldsmith and his girlfriend Candice slumbered on. Tall and rakish with long mousey hair, Andy was the son of a wealthy industrialist, who to his parent's joy had sailed through Eton and Cambridge and had been sent down with a first-class honour's degree in law and economics. After finishing university, Andy decided that he needed space to 'find himself' and had decided to travel, meeting Candi, as she preferred to be called, a thin, tanned, brown-haired nymphomaniac from Hastings, in Thailand. Candi introduced the sexually and worldly naïve Andy to the delights of the Kama Sutra as well as a variety of chemical and herbal substances that Andy took to with relish.

It didn't take long for the neat and proper Andrew, as his mother called him, to transform into Spud, Candi's pet name for him into every bit the new-age traveller. Long hair, scruffy clothes and questionable bathing habits. He loved it. Andy's new quest in life was to find a solution to world peace and the longer he remained stoned, the closer he thought he was to solving the problem. Forays into Buddhism, Hinduism, Krishna and Weight Watchers in addition to the odd cult here and there had left him baffled and confused and swift retreats into bouts of prolonged chemical abuse usually did the trick to further cloud the issue.

Certain that the world was doomed despite his best efforts, Spud prepared himself for Armageddon.

After shagging and doping themselves across much of Southeast Asia, the pair had returned to the UK to follow the pop music festival circuit and were on their way to Glastonbury. Still heavily under the influence of last night's narcotic feast, Candi came to first and as usual, went straight for Spud's todger. "Wake up, Spud," she giggled into his ear while trying to instil some life into his little old man by tugging at it. "Come on, babe, wake up I need shagging," Candi's hunger for all things carnal was legendary and had been the reason behind her being expelled from one of the top girls boarding schools. No one should enjoy being caned or misbehaving atrociously in order to be caned is not natural, the principal had written in his letter to her parents asking them to collect her from the school immediately.

Spud roused himself to find Candi already bouncing up and down on his semi-erect manhood. Although Candi was Spud's first sexual partner in the short time, they had known each other he had more than made up for his late start. As Candi's skinny torso writhed excitedly trying to pump a little more life into Spud's 'thingy' as she sometimes referred to it, Spud's head protruded from inside the tent.

Confronted by the black mass of cloud and ash enveloping the site, the small explosions sending sparks and flash into the sky and minute mushroom clouds and flames from Dave's barbeque on the other side of the hedge, Spud couldn't believe his eyes. "Fucking amazing man," he whispered, "fucking far out, brother." Goodness knows how his drug-ravaged brain was interpreting the cataclysmic scene he was watching. Complete environmental collapse or a spiritual event, who knows? With his eyes fixed on the spectacle above and Candi on top of him squealing with sexual delight, it seemed the end of the world was about to happen and not half as bad as he imagined it would be.

"Doggy, doggy," implored Candi, "do it doggy doggy," she hopped off his now fully erect todger and thrust her rear end in the air inviting his entrance. Spud took up position behind Candi and started to perform and they soon ended up outside of the tent consumed by erotic delight and unaware of anything other than their carnal lust.

Across from their tent, all the squealing and writhing about had attracted the attention of a huge St Bernard dog called Francis, owned by Bob and Margaret Owens, permanent summer residents at Happy Trails who usually spent the summer months enjoying the peaceful setting Happy Trails is. As everyone knew them and in turn Francis the dog had the freedom to roam around the site at will.

Up until now, the most exciting thing Francis came across was the occasional squirrel which no longer held any interest at all as he was far too old now to give a decent chase. The sight of this strange long-haired couple doing what comes naturally interested Francis so much that he wandered across to see what was going on. Staring at this strange couple lustfully intertwined and oblivious to his presence and without any hesitation was up on his hind legs placing two huge hairy paws on Spud's shoulders panting furiously into Spud's ear and drooling down Spud's back trying to join in.

Averting his attention from Candi momentarily, Spud was suddenly aware he was about to take a severe rogering from a huge black dog.

"Fuck off, Lassie," wailed Spud clenching his buttocks as hard as he could, "go on fuck off," but the huge black dog continued to try and take up position to consummate this unholy relationship despite Spud's best efforts to dislodge him.

In the meantime, Candi was having the ride of her life as Spud gyrated back and forth trying to dislodge Francis. All the bad language was having an extremely erotic effect and she wondered why they had never tried this before. "More, more," begged Candi urging Spud on. "Get the fuck off me," cried Spud shaking his bum furiously from side to side. "But baby, I don't want you to stop," begged Candi.

Francis was beginning to like this game, it made him feel like a puppy again, although he was beginning to tire of Spud's hard-to-get attitude and unwillingness to succumb, so decided to give one last big push before losing interest. With all his weight bearing down on Spud's shoulders Francis pushed forward sending all three of them crashing outside across the grass.

Quick as a flash, Spud was up on his feet cupping one hand on his bum and the other holding his bollocks trying to make his escape from this canine gigolo. Candi looked up in horror as she saw this huge black dog seemingly dismount her bloke. "You dirty bastard," she yelled at the retreating Spud, "If I knew you were into that sort of thing, I'd never have let you near me, you filthy dirty shitbag." Looking back in disbelief at Candi, Spud knew this wasn't the time for leaving one's naked rear end sticking up in the air, especially not with a slavering, sex-crazed 12-stone hairy canine on the loose.

Francis had also noticed Candi's skinny rear end and was making a beeline for it.

Spud saw Francis advancing on his unprotected Candi at speed and started a bare-foot blocking tactic. Francis saw Spud moving in to block his amorous advances, Candi saw a semi-erect Spud and a drooling and fixated Francis both seemingly bearing down on her. In slow motion, she watched as Spud launched himself into Francis hoping to knock him off course. "Noooooo," shouted Spud.

"Grrrrrrr," growled Francis, as all three again sprawled across the grass in a tangle of tits, bums, bollocks, flesh, drool and hair.

Margaret Owens opened her caravan door and rattled Francis's food bowl, "Where is that dog now?" She muttered. Francis hearing his master's call and with the prospect of food imminent decided that perhaps at his age, this game was no longer fun, so disentangled himself and trotted off.

Chapter 10: A Little Get-Together

As the sun shone brightly across Happy Trails and the majority of the campers were now settled into the holiday weekend, sleeping, playing games, exploring the site, the usual things campers do, Dan was preparing for the get-together and had already sorted out a table full of bottles of drink, a couple of coolers full of ice overflowing with cold American beer, well, the stuff made here that tastes fuck all like the real stuff, but it had the right labels. All the food was ready as were the barbeques, decent ones.

All that Dan needed now was the guests, most notably the American blonde bombshell.

As Tina was yet to appear, Dan wandered across to reception to be greeted by a dozen children buying sweets. "Tina, love, get these little fuckers to piss off," he gestured towards the kids who looked at him alarmingly. A couple of gobstoppers and a Curly Whirly wasn't going to stand in the way of Anglo-American relations, at least not the relations he had in mind.

Dan walked into the back office where a fridge full of booze was. "Drink, sweetheart?" He asked knowing full well she would have been having a sneaky one or two during quiet moments.

Pouring a very large measure of Negrita, a highly potent Spanish spirit, into a tumbler and mixing in a good measure of Polish vodka he topped it up with ice and gave the glass to Tina.

"Mister, can I have an ice cream?" A ginger-haired eight-year-old boy asked pointing at the freezer.

"Young man, you can go fuck snakes, now clear off," Dan said leaning menacingly over the scruffy child before gently but forcefully marshalling the boy out of the door.

Tina by now had downed most of the potent mixture and tried not to slur her words. "We'd better go, what time are the others coming, there's a lot to do?" She could never be sure as Dan might have already insulted or made crude enough suggestions to have put any potential guests off. "Of course, we are, dear, don't panic I've been preparing the food all afternoon, all I have to do is light the charcoal." Fantastic, thought Tina she'd have time to shower and sober up a bit. By the overpowering smell of cheap aftershave, it appeared Dan wasn't bothering to bathe, a wet wipe around the love spuds and dowsing himself in cheap aftershave would more than do.

Tina put a cigarette to her lips but stopped short of lighting it, the amount of alcohol she had consumed made her breath as flammable as petrol and the overpowering stench of Dan's aftershave mixed with her breath only exacerbated the risk.

Leaving the unlit cigarette between her lips, she closed the office door and weaved gently across the car park towards their caravan. Breathing in the fresh air deeply, the potency of her last drink was magnified, and she found herself a little light-headed.

Arriving shortly after Dan at their caravan, she could see Dan making small talk with the DiAngelos, especially Debbie

DiAngelo, Aaron and Tristan had also arrived, but no sign of Bob and Maud. Tina couldn't understand why Dan invited them as he couldn't stand Maud, the feeling was mutual, and he thought Bob was a wimp. It had to be the dominance thing where Dan could show everyone, he was the top dog in this field.

As the small gathering mingled, Dan invited his guests to help themselves to drinks and a selection of nibbles, he had arranged in plastic bowls.

Chuck took a cold Bud from the cooler; it tasted like cold piss and nothing like the Bud he gets back home, but it was a warm day and if this was the best the Brits could offer that would have to do.

"Allow me to get you a refreshment," Dan said creepily to Debbie, trying to keep his front false tooth in place.

"Oh, nuthin too strong, there partner." She giggled. "I ain't use to hard liquor," which was just what Dan wanted to hear as he poured a large measure of the foul-tasting Negrita into a glassful of ice and added another large measure of some of the cheapest whisky he had. Hard licker, he mused, I'm the best hard licker here.

All he had to do was get rid of Chuck and Tina out of the way.

Aaron helped himself to a couple of large glasses of white wine, one for him and one for Tristan. Although it was one step up from paint thinners in both taste and bouquet, if it was kept cold enough, it was passable. Dan on the other hand had been over imbibing with the decent scotch and chasing it down with super 8% strength cider most of the afternoon and his over familiarity tendencies were beginning to surface.

The gathering, now seated around the barbeques, was making small talk and exchanging niceties. "Chuck, my friend, try some of this, single grain, a small distillery on the West Coast of Scotland, one of my favourites," Dan proffered a very large tumbler of heavily laced cheap whisky to Chuck, who rather than offend his host downed half of it in a cavalier manner. Keeping it a) down and b) off his teeth, as the corrosive mixture settled the effects were almost instant. Chuck sat back heavily and coughed a little.

"Another?" Dan asked, whisking Chuck's half-empty tumbler out of his hand and swiftly topping it up. "Gee, thanks," said Chuck as Dan handed the overflowing tumbler back to him.

"Bottoms up, friends, across the water and all that," Dan held his glass up toasting his guests and draining the decent stuff from his glass.

"Oh, yeah, bottoms up," Chuck's now unsteady hand held out his glass.

Tina had forgotten about taking a full shower and had joined him in a wet wipe around the important bits, she could see that Dan's alcohol intake had reached an insulting level.

As the small talk slipped into a lull Dan seized the moment "Tell me, Aaron," said Dan leaning forward, "I've often wondered how gays like you pick up one another." Aaron looked warily at Tristan.

"Come again, Dan?" Aaron looked at Dan.

"Oh no, that's not the question for me, I'm not cumming again, but that is potentially, potentially," Dan gestured by swinging his spectacles by one arm, "the gist of my question," Dan smirked, his false front tooth resting on his bottom lip like a fang. Tina could see the afternoon was going downhill quicker than usual.

Dan continued, "You see what I don't understand is how poofs, you don't mind me calling you two poofs, do you? I mean you are poofs, benders, bum bandits or whatever you like to be called, how do you know who is a bummer and who is a bummee, you know the giver and the taker, the rider and the ridden, the sausage or the jockey?" With each adjective, Dan made various crude gestures.

Tina, Chuck and Debbie looked as stunned as Aaron and Tristan and tried to steer the conversation to another topic. "Any plans for the weekend, Debbie?" Tina's attempt at diverting the conversation was abruptly stopped.

Dan continued to get into his most adversarial crude stride. "It's a fair question, I think, I mean is there some sort of secret signal or a code word, after all, you would be well and truly in the shit if two bummee's got together." He couldn't help laughing at the use of his expletive in his question. Dan looked at Chuck, who by now was feeling the effects of most of the bottle of cheap, genuine scotch, and grinned. "Bet you don't have sausage jockeys in the Marines, eh," winked Dan.

The thought of sausages, especially in Dan's context was making him feel sick, or nauseous as the Yanks prefer to say, while the effects of Booby's potent aperitif was also having the desired effect as she undid a couple of buttons on her top revealing more of her voluptuous breasts. On seeing this, Dan's creative urges got the better of him and the need to extend his 'dicky pics' collection became a matter of urgency.

Sweating profusely, Dan turned the chicken and burgers over while using the corner of the barbeque to rub his dick on to release it from the confines of his boxer shorts. "Nearly there, I hope you're all hungry, back in a jiffy."

He slipped away walking awkwardly as his todger became more entangled in his underwear, Tina watched anxiously. Was he going to make another addition to his 'Dicky Pics?' She hoped he wasn't.

As suspected, Dan had headed back to the office. Sat in the semi-darkness of the back office, he whipped out his manhood. "I know, I'll lighten it up a bit," he chuckled pulling back his foreskin and with an indelible black marker drew two eyes, a nose and lips on the head of his flaccid penis. Pulling the foreskin halfway back, his penis had taken on the sinister appearance of a demonic hooded worm. Taking careful aim with his phone, he snapped a couple of shots, which in his drunken state made him laugh hysterically. A knock at the door brought him abruptly back to his senses. "Got any milk?" A voice from outside called.

"Bugger off, we're shut," replied, Dan not caring who it was on the other side of the door.

Looking up DiAngelo's contact number from the booking screen, which he dialled into his mobile phone and soon the newly taken 'Dicky Pics' were winging their way to the delightfully drunk Debbie. Unfortunately, in his inebriated state, he had also clicked Tina's mother's number and she too would soon be privy to pictures of the demonic worm.

Aaron sniffed the air, what was that acrid stench? He looked at the food cooking on Dan's setup, they looked ok, and he was sure the smell wasn't coming from that. Tristan grabbed his arm and pointed Aaron in the direction of Dave's caravan. "What the fuck is that?" He said as they both looked at the billowing smoke and ash that was once Dave's barbeque.

Whatever it was, it didn't look good and the choice between staying at the gathering to be ridiculed or attending the apocalypse was easy; the apocalypse beckoned.

Chapter 11: Desperate Measures

Dave now free of Carol's grasp cowered behind the caravan door. What the hell could he do to extinguish the inferno that threatened all mankind? Knock the fucker over, fragment the contents and that'll make it burn out quicker, he thought and convinced himself that this was a recognised fire-fighting practice. Dave's eyes swept the caravan looking for anything that he could use to send a salvo to unbalance the inferno. "Bugger all, absolutely bugger all," he said to himself before his eyes chanced upon Carol's culinary spread.

"Outa the way, fatso," Dave ordered elbowing Carol to one side and grabbing up at the Meetee burgers laid out on the table. Taking one and opening just the top section of the door, Dave took aim. Eyes narrowed to afford some protection from the heat radiating from the fire Dave launched the burger, Frisbee-like, at the inferno. "Bollocks missed," said Dave adjusting his stance a little before launching burger number 2. Just over the top. As Carol lay moaning on the floor, Dave lined up number 3. "Bingo," Dave shouted as burger 3 scored a direct hit sending a ball of hot ash and sparks into the air. Peering over the door Dave saw the inferno still standing, "Fuck it," he cursed.

Burger after burger sailed through the air until there were none left.

After 12 direct hits, the inferno stood upright and virtually intact and if it was possible getting worse. To accompany the hissing charcoal, Dave could now hear the fat content from the lips and bum burgers adding fuel to the inferno as they began to cook. For one moment, Dave sniffed the air, "Ah food," food, what was he thinking of? If his stupid bint of a wife hadn't bought the fucking thing in the first place, he wouldn't be in this mess now. He glanced around at Carol still comatose on the floor as another small explosion rocked the caravan.

Carol now slowly regaining consciousness crawled towards her darling Dave surprised at how comfortable her rear end felt considering the aftertaste of Sweet Martini lingering on her lips. "Dave, I'm sorry, I love you, Dave," her enforced nap had done nothing to fix her whining tone. Reaching out to feel where her man was, she caught hold of his exposed wedding tackle hanging from his shorts and without thinking heaved herself up. Dave yelped in pain as he felt his todger being forcibly elongated. Dave swiped at Carol's hand trying to get her to relinquish her vice-like grip. "Let it go, bitch, let it go, let go of my dick, for fuck's sake," screamed Dave as his face reddened in anger and considerable pain. Flames continued to track ferociously heavenwards just as Dave was fully expecting his manhood to be totally torn off Carol finally released his molested member taking the remnants of his shorts.

"Where are my fucking clothes?" He rasped.

"Still in the case," responded a tearful Carol. Without any hesitation, Dave pulled a brand-new sheet from the freshly made bed and wrapped it around his sooty black torso while reaching down to retrieve the remains of his shorts which he put on his head to protect what was left of his singed hair.

Dave pulled the tray of uncooked chicken legs from the counter to the floor. This'll do it, thought Dave taking aim with the chicken leg at the inferno. Launching the poultry projectile with as much force as his panic fatigued body could summon, Dave watched as the leg flew, and once again bounced off the inferno. More force was needed. "Carol, get up, come on, you lazy fat bitch, get up." Dave shook her fully back to consciousness. Carol looked up at Dave, he had called her Carol, actually called her Carol, feelings of love raced through her body for the first time since this fiasco began. Dave knelt beside her. "Right, listen the fuck up, we haven't got much time, if we both throw a chicken leg at the same time, it'll double up the force and knock that fucking thing over, and another thing while I think about it, if you ever buy me anything ever again, I swear I'll kill you with my bare hands, got it, fatty?" Carol had, although there was probably a better way of saying it.

So, Dave wrapped in a sheet and bare-breasted Carol stood in the half-opened door armed to the teeth or in Carol's case tits, with chicken legs. "Fire," roared Dave like a gunnery commander as two chicken legs were hurled towards the barbeque.

It rocked, slightly, but it rocked. They were onto something with this line of attack.

"Quick, reload," Dave barked. Carol pulled a puzzled face, reload, reload what? What was she missing here?

"Reload dammit, reload, it's rocking," screamed Dave with a palpable frenzy in his voice. With that, the pair launched a fresh poultry salvo and watched as the barbeque tilted to one side, rocked and then stopped, tilted at an almost impossible angle. "Bollocks, there's only one thing for it," Dave shouted and screamed like a madman as he exited the safety of the caravan and bounded towards the mass with a plastic snow shovel and jabbed furiously at the half-tilted mass, just in time to be seen by Spud fleeing from the sex-crazed Francis. "Oh, fuck me drunk, this doesn't look good," thought Spud now doubling back on himself away from the lunatic in a dress.

In the near distance, the wail of a siren could be heard.

"Oh, thank you, Lord," extolled Dave as he was sure that help by way of the fire brigade had arrived.

Chapter 12: Here Comes the Cavalry

At the gate, Constable Thomas pulled up in his patrol car, sirens wailing and blue lights flashing, he jumped out and surveyed the scene. A recent call alerting him to a major incident at Happy Trails had been a much-welcome distraction from sitting in a lay-by waiting for speeding drivers.

At first glance, there didn't appear to be anything untoward, yes there was lots of smoke, but on any given summer bank holiday, the number of barbeques blazing away gave an almost blitz-like atmosphere.

Running towards him he could see a naked man doing his best to conceal his wedding tackle with hands cupping his bits in front of him.

"You'd better come quick, are you armed?" A frantic Spud asked now pulling at Thomas's shirt. "This way and for fucks sake hurry, where's the rest of you?" Thomas pulled back from Spud's frantic grasp.

"Hold on, hold on, I got a call to say there was a lunatic terrorist on the loose," said Thomas looking squarely at Spud.

"There is, over there where the ash and shit are billowing up, I've seen him, dressed in robes with a turban on, he's armed as well, screaming and shouting in some foreign language," Spud's ranting was enough for Thomas to know there had to be something in Spud's story.

"Who's in charge around here?" Thomas asked.

"Fuck knows I'm not," Spud briefly wondered why Thomas would ask such a stupid question. Thomas looked disgusted at the thought of searching the naked Spud. Seeing the reception, Thomas tried the door, locked, Thomas looked for an out-of-hours procedure or contact number, and finding it, he proceeded to dial it.

Tina answered the call, still light-headed from her earlier drinking session she was shocked that on a sunny bank holiday, the police were at the gates. "What's wrong?" A puzzled Tina asked.

"Terrorists," replied Thomas. It still didn't make sense.

"Is my husband there?" Tina asked.

"Listen, love, even if there was someone here, I don't know who your husband is, what's his name?"

Just as Tina was giving Thomas Dan's name, the office door opened and a sweaty Dan appeared in the doorway, he stared at Thomas nervously. Surely to shit Debbie DiAngelo hasn't called the old bill in, had she? Dan had to think fast. Thomas now confronted with a guilty-looking Dan wondered why the owner of the site was emerging from the office with a black stain covering the front of his trousers in the zipper area and switched his gaze several times between Dan's eyes and his crotch, making Dan all the more uncomfortable. "Leaky pen," said Dan gesturing to the stain and hoping he'd remembered to do his zipper up, "Fucking thing, leaked everywhere." Thomas wasn't looking for explanations.

"You in charge of this place?" Thomas asked pointedly.

"That's right, Dan O'Connor, I own the place, why?"

"Had reports of a terrorist attack, this bloke says there's an armed lunatic dressed in robes and wearing a turban shouting and carrying on." It was Dan's turn to look confused.

"You sure, constable, I mean this isn't Beirut, it's Happy Trails, we don't get many terrorists in this neck of the woods."

"Whether you do or whether you don't, I've had a report and I'm here to investigate," Thomas sounded official.

"On your own?" Dan said looking beyond the constable for backup and forgetting the black stain on his trousers. "A lunatic terrorist, what was it, crazed madman, and you're here on your own, unarmed, not even a decent truncheon?" Thomas had to admit on a scale of 1 to 10 in anti-terrorist responses, he was scoring very badly.

"Well, I'm all you've got, so we'll have to make do," Thomas wasn't instilling confidence and Dan would rather he fucked off ASAP so that he could return to this afternoon's perving.

"Look, constable, this is obviously a police matter, so if I could leave it to you and laddo here," Dan gestured towards the naked Spud, "I have a small gathering to attend and I'm late." Dan hadn't chosen his words well. Spud now standing with his hands on his hips forgetting his total lack of attire looked alarmed.

"Fuck you, Baldy, I'm a lover, not a fighter, you go with the pig and sort it out, and I'm off," and Spud quickly but cautiously made his way back towards his tent and the irate Candi, hoping that by now she'd have wiped the image of Francis from her memory.

A few miles along the coast is Camp Biddington, once a fortress against the invader, but that was a long time ago.

Nowadays rather than echo the rumble of a great war machine, the setting was picture-perfect tranquillity. Beautifully manicured lawns with flowerbeds displaying a riot of colourful plants were more Chelsea Flower Show than a bastion of aggression. At the entrance heavy green painted iron gates still displayed huge signs proclaiming 'Home of the tank regiment' with the regiment's insignia emblazoned brightly underneath, alongside the fifteen-foot-high walls perfectly positioned half whisky barrels burgeoned with spectacular shrubs.

In the wardroom at Camp Biddington, Sergeant Eddie Jones answered the phone, "Wardroom, Sergeant Jones speaking, can I help you?"

On the other end of the line was Constable Wayne Thomas, "Constable Thomas here, Sussex Constabulary, quick we need your help at Happy Trails the campsite just along the coast."

Jones could hear there was an urgency and desperation in Constable Thomas's voice.

"And what sort of help would that be constable?" Jones enquired.

"Terrorist attack," responded Thomas bluntly. Jones frowned, in all his 19 years in the army he had never had a call like this. Pushing his beret back from his forehead, he looked up at a detailed map of the area trying to pinpoint where Happy Trails was. "Hello, constable am I hearing you right, terrorist attack at Happy Trails?"

"Correct," replied Thomas, "or affirmative, or whatever you military blokes say."

"Correct is good enough, constable, why do you think it's a terrorist attack?" Jones frowned, a terrorist attack on the long summer bank holiday, in Sussex, this must be a hoax. "Look, constable, if you are a constable, how can I be sure you're not some nutter trying to wind me up?" Thomas had to think on his feet.

"Go outside and take a look, you must be able to see the smoke from there," he implored. Jones put down the receiver on the desk and went outside. Just as Thomas described, there was a thick bloom of black smoke hanging over where Happy Trails should be. Returning to the wardroom, Jones picked up the receiver, "Ok, constable, what do you want me to do?" Jones still uncertain and very puzzled wondered what Thomas was going to suggest.

Thomas growing in frustration at Jones' lack of urgency replied, "How about sending some troops with a tank or two before this shit storm gets any worse and the country is overthrown?" This made Jones start to lose his temper. "Excuse me, constable, but do you know who you are calling?"

"Of course, I bloody do, the army, the tank regiment to be exact," Thomas wasn't sure why Jones was even asking that question.

What Thomas didn't know was that although Camp Biddington was part of the tank regiment, it was no longer an active part of it. Tanks were no longer based at Camp Biddington and there weren't any troops either. As far as the army was concerned, Camp Biddington was virtually dormant, they didn't exist. No one visited the camp, no one called the camp; they hadn't seen any top brass for years.

"Jones, why are you wasting time, get the tanks rolling and bring plenty of blokes, we'll need them," barked Thomas down the line hoping to instil some urgency into the matter.

"Look, sorry, constable, you don't understand, I haven't got any tanks or any blokes and certainly no ammo to send you, there's nothing here, they mothballed us years ago, I've been here 15 years and there weren't any tanks here back then, it's just me, Corporal Percy, Privates Smith and Brown." At Seventy-Eight Corporal, Percy was well past retirement age and had so far clocked up sixty-two years active service, longer than any man in today's modern army, as were Privates Smith and Brown, sixty-one and sixty-three respectively.

Forgotten about by the War Office and still drawing pay, they all enjoyed life on the coast. Every day was a gardening day.

Usually, starting their day around 09:30 with a good feed, they would then venture out and tend to the lawns and flowerbeds of Camp Biddington, which looked exceptionally beautiful this year, a real credit for their efforts and to the battalion.

Thomas staggered back, not daring to believe what Jones was telling him.

Jones continued, "Look, constable, the last time we had anyone come here was two sausage jockeys from the Civil Service in Whitehall, they thought the tank regiment was full of Nancy boys so they came down here looking to have some err, you know, fun! I told them straight if you'll excuse the pun, we don't hold with that liggitbitiqy stuff here, so I told the pair to go, excuse the language, fuck themselves, which oddly enough I think they did, anyway the last I saw was them heading off Brighton way, never saw them again or anyone else."

Thomas cut in, "But we need help, what can you do, Jones, don't you understand what's happening?" In the background, Jones heard what he thought to be an explosion.

"Look constable, I'll tell you what we've got at our disposal, I've got a gun turret from a WW2 tank, can't move it though it weighs six tons and Corporal Percy has just finished the flower borders around it and a rather fetching pansy and begonia display along the barrel, there's a caterpillar track off something else, I can't remember what, but it's buggered anyway, a nearly complete set of spark plugs off an armoured car, I say nearly complete as I used a couple in my car, work a treat they do."

"Jones, for heaven's sake, where are all the tanks?" Thomas couldn't believe what Jones was saying, nothing but scraps.

Now getting irritated with Thomas's line of questioning, Jones replied curtly, "Where are ALL the tanks, ALL, there isn't that much ALL to be had, let's see, the PM has promised fourteen sodding tanks to that shindig in Eastern Europe, they'll be fucking lucky, we haven't got fourteen in working order, so sending the shit we have to the shit show out there will just make it a shittier shit show than the shit show it currently is it and would be better off without the shit we've got to offer, we could muster up two, maybe, perhaps, as long as they don't expect to use them in anger, now there's two on display at the Imperial War Museum that have no engines or working munitions systems, there's another one stuck on Bodmin Moor, has been for ten years now, so totally fucked and I believe there's one at Buckingham Palace, but don't quote me on that. That's it, constable, our tank capability unless they've bought some new ones but that's unlikely."

"But what about all those photos and films of our tanks rolling across the countryside?" Thomas asked.

"Propaganda, ruskies, Yanks, all faked, photoshopped, I think you call it, we haven't had a tank regiment in years, well not since the Second World War and that's before my time, tell you what, we have a milk float here, I swapped some old uniforms and tools for it a couple of years ago, we use it to move the lawnmowers around the camp, I could ask the boys if they'd come over and take a shufty at your situation, I'm not promising mind you, the boys were looking at a bit of a picnic on the beach seeing it's a bank holiday."

Take a shufty, a fucking shufty, the terrorists are trying to overrun Happy Trails and all this prick is offering is three OAPs to come and take a shufty. Thomas was lost for words. No tanks, no soldiers, no credible response. Looking at his options, he mentally ran through the resources he had at his disposal.

In all, he had nothing to work with.

"Ok, Jones, send what you have but be prepared for a fight, things could get really messy," with that, Thomas hung up.

"I'll try HQ one more time," he said to himself and rang the main police station. "It's Thomas from Area 51 patrol," he said to the operator at HQ, "I need help, urgent help, we've got a terrorist attacking Happy Trails camping site and I need armed backup immediately." Thomas summed up the situation concisely.

"Really, dear, calm down," came the reply. "You do know what day it is, don't you?" There appeared to be the same lack of response at HQ as there was from Camp Biddington. "No, what day is it?" A puzzled Thomas asked.

"Honestly, you beat bobbies, you're all the same, it's the Gay Pride Rally in Brighton, you aren't expecting anybody to be here, are you, we've been working all week on decorating the panda cars in rainbow bunting and balloons, Inspector Reece has issued all bobbies with rainbow waistcoats, hats and whistles, he's outdone himself this year and got a face paint artist to paint all the bobbies faces with Pride rainbows, most of the force is already on the police float dancing and blowing kisses, DI Morgan has cut the bum cheek pieces out of his uniform trousers, he's such a laugh, I'm surprised you didn't get the memo."

Thomas couldn't quite comprehend what he was being told.

"And what do I do about the terrorist attack?" He asked.

"I don't know, we're committed to inclusivity, gay rights, investigating hate crimes or people upset at hurtful words, but fighting terrorists isn't on the agenda," replied the operator.

"Taliban, Mujahedeen, for fucks sake, you must have heard of them?" The conversation was taking a direction that Thomas would rather not take.

"Listen, potty mouth, Tallington, Taliban or whatever you're on about, nothing comes between the force and Gay Pride weekend, understand, nothing," the operator was obviously fed up with dealing with matters of national security.

"You'll be fucking sorry when this shit hits the nationals," muttered Thomas hoping that something would sink in with this woman.

"Oi, listen to me, Thomas, you start with those straight threats with me, and I'll have the equalities commission on you." Thomas wondered if this was a woman he was speaking to.

"Ok, love," he said testing the waters. "Love, you cheeky bastard." Thomas was now sure the effeminate voice on the other end of the line was a bloke, sort of.

"So that's it then, the country is being overrun with blood-crazed terrorists and all you can tell me is the entire force is doing the gay quick step around Brighton dressed in rainbow waistcoats and hats and DI Morgan has his arse out?"

The phone went dead.

Thomas now realised that far from screwing up, any gay-related memos in the future he really should take them more seriously and headed back to his panda car.

Chapter 13: Family Matters

Dan stumbled back to the gathering pleased with the outcome of his pictorial endeavours, he was expecting the delightful Debbie to have downloaded it and be in the mood for more, much more. In his drunken state, the more he thought about what he had done; the more he thought that any amorous advance he made towards Debbie, the more it would be reciprocated.

As he was approaching, he caught sight of Debbie entering his caravan, probably to use the facilities, but to Dan, it was her scanning the area for a safe place to pull a few strokes with him. Picking up the pace, he hurried to the rear of his caravan onto the decked area that ran around the outside. Through the slightly ajar toilet window, he could hear movement inside. It must be Debbie; she must have seen him approaching and gone inside.

What was happening inside the toilet was Debbie throwing up all the cheap alcohol Dan had given her earlier. Dan leant towards the open window, "Hellooo, helloohooo," he softly whispered through the small gap to alert Debbie he was there. Debbie, heaving up the last of the foul mixture hadn't heard Dan's calling. Dan assumed that Debbie was keeping quiet so that their little dalliance wouldn't be overheard so dropped his jeans and boxers.

Standing on tiptoes he could just about poke the demonic worm through the small gap, hoping Debbie would oblige with an oral massage.

He couldn't have been further from the truth!

Debbie now finished vomiting, looked up from the toilet bowl at the open window with Dan's demonic worm-like penis sticking through.

Dan saw movement and anticipated the imminent sexual encounter.

Debbie screamed and slumped back against the toilet sending a small judder through the bathroom, but enough to make the window close on Dan's erect member. Startled, Dan immediately tried withdrawing his rapidly drooping willy out of the window only to find the sharp edges had trapped it; the more he tried to withdraw, the more the window was pulled shut, which meant if he withdrew it any further, a non-medical instant circumcision, that could have removed both foreskin and head, was highly likely. He had to think of something quickly as his leg muscles were now in danger of locking up having spent so long on tiptoes. If he pushed the window open to release his todger, Debbie was certain to see it was him and judging by her reaction to his somewhat crude advances so far, perhaps he hadn't quite wooed her enough or read the mood music correctly. If he stayed trapped in the circumcision stance, Tina and Chuck were bound to catch him and he couldn't see that ending well either.

Maybe it was the alcohol, maybe it was the sight of that horrible appendage sticking through the window glaring at her with its black lifeless staring eyes; whatever it was, it was too much, and Debbie passed out.

"Oh, fuck me drunk," said Dan panicking, seeing Debbie pass out he pushed the window open releasing his now bruised, but flaccid penis.

Pulling his willy out of the window, he jumped off the decking, rolled under it and lay still hiding and waiting to see what happened next. He could hear Tina and Chuck consoling Debbie. He cocked his head to hear what was being said.

Debbie was rambling about a deformed snake with an evil face trying to get through the window. "Hideous, horrible evil snake, dripping mouth, coming closer," Debbie was on the verge of hysteria.

"Snake," Dan looked at his willy, still hanging out of his unzipped jeans, "Snake," he was pleased with that part of her description. Python would have been better, but he'd settle for a snake. As all the attention was focussed on Debbie, Dan took the opportunity to roll away and make good his escape from the scene. Circling low around a few caravans, Dan doubled back and took a fresh approach to his caravan.

Turning the corner, he saw Tina appearing to console Debbie and Chuck looking wild with rage. Tina had her phone to her ear, and he could hear, even at a distance, the angry voice of his mother-in-law.

His plan obviously wasn't working out as he thought it would. Quick thinking and a new plan were required.

Changing pace and heading determinedly back to his caravan Dan met Tina, Debbie and Chuck head-on. Tina, seeing Dan headed in his direction. "You dirty bastard, my mother, my mother, Dan what did she ever do to deserve that? and Debbie, a guest, why?" Tina brushed her long brown hair back from her face, he could see the rage in her eyes. Of all the things he had done in the past, nothing was as bad as this, her mother! Dan's mind raced, her mother, what about her mother; he couldn't stand her mother, worming, excuse the pun, out of this was going to take a monumental effort.

The incident that had brought the police to his site and ruined his plans, he needed to make into something of huge importance. Dan didn't really care about whatever was happening on the site as whatever it was it couldn't be a terrorist attack, even if it was it'd soon go away, and Dan could get back to doing his usual bugger all.

"Tina, stop, whatever you're on about, stop," Dan spoke with authority that usually disarmed Tina, out of the corner of his eye Dan caught sight of the enraged Chuck bearing down on him. Dan held his hand up, "Right listen up, we have a serious issue to deal with and there's no time to lose." The only issue Chuck had on his mind was cutting off Dan's demonic worm and shoving it down Dan's throat. Dan was confronted by Chuck towering over him. Holding Dan by the throat he pulled him up, so they were face to face and given that Chuck was at least a foot taller than Dan meant Dan's feet were off the floor and swinging helplessly.

"Chuck, put me down, I need your help, terrorist attack." Perhaps it was the sense of duty or a whiff of Dan's lack of oral hygiene that stopped Chuck dead in his tracks, and he released Dan, dropping him to the floor.

Tina, Debbie and Chuck looked menacingly at Dan waiting for an explanation.

Dan, ignoring all three, went to a small storage unit behind his caravan and rummaged around emerging with a garden rake, a spade, a large broom and a watering can. "It's not much but it's the best I can do," he said as he distributed the gardening implements to each of them. "Right, over there," Dan nodded towards the hedge separating the two fields, "we have a terrorist running wild, he's already set off some explosive device and the next thing on his list is, I'll bet, to murder people." Tina looked bewildered, even for Dan this was too much, just how low could he go to cover up his weird pursuits?

"Ok, Chuck, you're the experienced one, so you should lead." Dan pointed to the pall of smoke which Chuck felt compelled to investigate. If anything should happen to Chuck, Dan was sure he'd be able to console Debbie, in one way or another!

Chuck, taking on a patrol stance, signalled with his hands to follow him and for the combat untrained or unready, Tina, Debbie and Dan, holding up the rear, instinctively followed. Chuck edged closer and could hear someone rambling in a strange language. In his military career, Chuck had picked up a few foreign words here and there so listened intently to see if this was a tongue, he was familiar with.

"Fucking bloody fuck fuck shit," said the Wildman. "Oh shit to shit, shit bollocks, ouch bastard shit my foot," not any dialect Chuck was versed in.

Chuck looked through a gap in the hedge and turned back to the others crouching silently behind him, "Tali-fucking-ban men, Tali-fucking-ban," Chuck whispered, narrowing his eyes while making a pointing motion towards the source of the ramblings. Dan lit up another cigarette.

"Any recommendations, Rambo?" Dan asked. Chuck considered the options. With no weapons, no ammunition, no backup and largely no idea, he was as fucked as the rest of them. Chuck looked back to the Wildman and caught sight of a hysterical Carol standing in the caravan doorway.

Chuck turned to his troops, his face serious, chin jutting out in front of his strong square jaw. "Oh no, he's got a hostage, a woman, he's got her naked, evil bastard, probably a sex slave," with that, Dan took an immediate interest, sex slave, sounded like fun! Dan strained his neck to get a better view, while Tina looked disgusted.

Chuck signalled to Tina, holding up his index finger and then pointing at her as if to signal her place in the manoeuvre was number one; he then made a circular motion with his arm and pointed to where her new position should be, closer to the mad man. Tina looked at Chuck startled to think she could take up 'point' armed with only a yard broom, she leant a little closer to Chuck and hoarsely whispered, "Fuck you, who the fuck do you think I am, this is a bloody brush, not an anti-tank gun?" Tina wasn't about to go toe-to-toe with any sodding terrorist, not even if the yard broom was new. Chuck had a rethink, turning to Dan he made the same gestures, but with a bit more emphasis. Dan frowned, as far as he was concerned Chuck could go fuck himself and ignoring Chuck's signals drew heavily on his cigarette and sat on his watering can. He had lost all faith in the leaders of the Free World.

"Fuck me drunk that's fucking hot, shit to fuck that hurts, oh for fuck sake my feet," screamed the Wildman. Chuck's attention was refocussed on the issue.

"I think he's calling for backup, I've heard that call before," as far as Dan was concerned the terrorist could call who the fuck he liked, Dan was only interested in the semi-naked woman.

"Where's our guy?" Chuck queried. "Who's that?"

Dan replied nonchalantly, "Taliban man,"

Chuck hissed, "Oh him, err over there somewhere, where's his bird, still got her tits out?" Dan's interest in the terrorist had hit an all-time low.

Dan slid the watering can underneath his head having completely lost any interest in the terrorist and finished his cigarette. The afternoon hadn't gone as planned, which quite frankly pissed him off, his intended dalliance with Mrs DiAngelo was a complete rubout and after this little fiasco was over, he had Tina to contend with and was trying to recall exactly when the dubious pictures had been sent to her mother. Last week, last month, surely not today.

Chuck on the other hand was completely focussed on the situation, even if his troop had lost interest, he was duty-bound to complete his mission. Something caught his attention, carefully making his way towards the scene was a man in uniform, a policeman, totally unarmed, but it was backup, of a sort. "Reinforcements, a copper," he said quietly and continued with hand gestures to signal the location of the copper.

"Really?" Dan rolled over, supporting himself on one elbow and pulling a blade of grass out stuck it in his teeth.

"There, over there, by that bush," Chuck pointed to where Constable Thomas was hiding. Dan took an uninterested look. "Oh, that prick, he'll get us all killed, never done anything more heroic than rescue the odd cat stuck up a tree, good fucking luck with that fella, I thought they'd got rid of him, fucking jobsworth." With that, Dan lit another cigarette and went back to resting his head on the watering can and pondering as to how a perfectly planned day had gone so badly wrong.

As Thomas made his way through the undergrowth, and did his best not to be seen, Chuck who was now in full ambush mode tried catching his attention. Cupping his hands around his mouth, he raised his head, "Hoot, hoooot, hoot, hoooooot," Chuck attempted that old tried and tested Indian method of owl calling.

Dan looked at Chuck, rolled his eyes and tutted, "Oh, for five fucking minutes, is that it? Do you really think that'll work? For fuck's sake, you're a Yank, think of something better." Chuck had killing Dan.

Thomas cocked his head, was that the old Indian owl call he was hearing? And immediately responded with, "Quack, quackkk, quack, quackkkk."

Chuck on hearing Thomas's response replied to confirm allegiance, "Hoot, hoooooot, hoot, hoooooot."

Dan shook his head, how the fuck did this idiot pull a bird like Debbie, he must have a prick like a baby's arm because intelligence it wasn't. Thomas, hearing that there was backup, even if it turned out to be a barn owl, belly shuffled towards Chuck's position.

On seeing Chuck, Thomas raised himself up to a semi-crouching position. "Constable Thomas, local constabulary," Thomas held out his hand. Chuck reciprocated holding out a huge hand and the pair shook hands like allies. "DiAngelo, Master Sergeant, United States Marine Corps."

Dan grimaced, raised his eyes and shook his head, "For fucks sake, are you two planning on doing anything constructive?" Looking through the hedge, Dan could see the crazy man still jabbing at the inferno and thought that was not going to end well.

Chuck and Thomas discussed a plan, a bloody silly one, but neither had ever been confronted with a situation requiring a forceful response. There followed a lot of gesturing, pointing, circling, and killing motions, but not any action.

Dan got to his feet, bored with all the inaction had decided to make a move of his own. "Fuck this for a game of soldiers, I'll sort it out," and with that, he pushed through the hedge, watched by Thomas, Chuck, Debbie and Tina. He marched towards Dave, who was still trying to knock the barbeque over while dancing bare foot on hot ashes.

"Oi, fella, yeh you, what the fuck are you doing?" Dan shouted at the crazed Dave. "Just look at this fucking mess you've made, that's going to cost you cleaning all that shit up."

As he approached, he could make out the large motherly breasts of Carol in the caravan doorway, "Fuck me, she's got a fair old pair on her." Dan was impressed. "Don't worry, love, I'll have you out of there in a jiffy, I'll just deal with this prick first." Dan didn't understand the response.

"Dave, darling, look, help coming," Carol yelled at Dave.

Dan looked around. "Who the fuck was Dave and where is this help?"

Dave now stood face to face with Dan. His sooty black face and body covered with a bedsheet and the remnants of his shorts on his head, "Mum, bloody fucking quefire," Dave pointed at the inferno trying to convey to Dan that this was what remained of his barbeque. Dan didn't understand what this madman was saying, but to err on the side of caution kicked him in the bollocks and nutted him for good measure.

"Oh you, fucking horrible bloody shit house," Dave groaned as his legs started to give way. Just to be sure that the crazy man wasn't going to retaliate, Dan punched him squarely in the face.

Carol screamed at Dan, "That's my husband, you bastard, leave him alone." Well now Dan could see the picture clearly, the fat bird with tremendous jugs, liked a bit of Arab cock, here he was risking life and limb and all this fat bird was thinking about was a bit of middle eastern knobbing.

He'd make sure this didn't happen ever again on his site and made a mental note to tell Tina no more interracial stuff here, great jugs or not.

Thomas, Chuck, Debbie and Tina, looked at Dan and were in awe of his actions. Single-handedly Dan had taken on the full force of a crazed terrorist and won. They all stood looking at Dan and his defeated adversary, now struggling to get to his feet.

Dan turned to look at his admiring followers, flexing his arms and kissing his biceps in an animated way.

Just as Dave got to his feet, Dan took him by the arm as the barbeque finally reached the point of no return and exploded sending Dan and Dave sailing through the air.

Then silence.

The sort of silence that follows a loud noise.

Nothing.

Tina and Debbie screamed.

Carol, stood in quiet disbelief, fixated on the scene.

Chuck and Thomas hurried to where Dan had fallen.

Dan had landed by the pensioners' rally tent, while Dave landed behind some bushes, a little further on.

As they approached through the smoke, they could see Dan getting to his feet, apparently none the worse for the experience, probably due to the amount of alcohol he had consumed earlier.

Dave was nowhere to be seen. Chuck pointed to the general direction that he thought the crazy man had landed and he and Thomas ran towards it. "Get him, before he takes more hostages," Chuck shouted.

Dave had cleared the bushes and had landed in an animal water trough in an adjacent field, unharmed other than having the tatty sheet blown clean off his body. He emerged a good deal cleaner, if not a lot smellier.

He stood dazed and naked, wondering what had just happened.

Thomas, fearing the worst jumped the five-bar gate into the field expecting to be greeted by either a dead man or a lunatic, but instead, there was a naked white man looking at a water trough.

"Where did he go; did you see which way he went?" Thomas asked. Dave said nothing, still trying to comprehend what was happening.

Thomas tried again, "A bloke in an Arab dishdasha and turban thing, did you see where he went?" It was no good, Dave had no idea what this policeman was asking and sat down gingerly on the edge of the trough.

Thomas looked at the naked Dave, "Exactly what are you doing, roaming about the place, you know, naked, tackle out, this isn't a bloody nudist site you know?"

Dave looked down at his bits hanging freely on display and slowly the past 15 minutes came back to him, along with the consequences of being identified as the mad man.

Dave thought quickly, "Oh him," he murmured, "the bloke with the thingy on and the head dress thing, he went across the field, pushed me in the trough as he went past, stole my clothes, he was armed you know." Dave thought, *stop now before you say too much and give the game away.*

Thomas reached for his radio and called into HQ.

"WhoooHoooo," said the operator in an affected voice, "Cheers for queers," whoever this was answering the phone they were pissed.

"It's Thomas, I called earlier about the terrorist attack. We've handled the situation, but the suspect has fled the scene, I need the helicopter up to track him."

On the other end of the line PC Flower, better known as Daisy to his colleagues and half of Brighton's gay scene, chatted merrily away. "Oh, you won't get that, dear, it's here, we're doing 'Ride the Chopper' trips for free." Thomas slumped back in the seat of his panda car. Daisy Flower went on, "There's a 'Do you want to Play with my Truncheon' tent, there's a queue a mile long for that, as you'd expect, it's so popular around here!" No, Thomas didn't expect, that riding the chopper and playing with my truncheon would be popular. What would be popular with the ratepayers of the South Coast would be some good old-fashioned coppering, blokes on the beat, arresting wrong doers, not prancing about blowing kisses and taking people on dubiously named rides.

"Where's the inspector?" Thomas knew this was a stupid question, but he had to ask. "Oh him, if I can call him 'him,' he's judging the 'Miss Trannie Midget' competition, I'm looking after his uniform, I couldn't make him out in all that pink and rainbow stuff, he's in no state to be buggering about chasing purple traitors, oh dear, I said purple traitors, how silly of me." Daisy was well and truly pissed, lost in a world of rainbows, pink bunting and hairy blokes in frocks. There wasn't a police station on the South Coast that was 'manned' today. The entire force lost in one huge gay hedonistic orgy.

Thomas hung up. It was a fool's errand to try and get a response.

He could see the headlines now. "Police ground helicopter as part of cost-cutting measures, 'Stations Close in Multi-Million Reorganisation Plan'." He looked around the site, there was nothing to be gained from staying there. The owners clearly didn't care, most of the other campers weren't even aware of what had happened, everything seemed normal, whatever that was for the place.

He closed the car door and went to find Dan. He could see Dan being cuddled by Tina, her man had defeated the foe and despite her knowing that it was Dan that had been responsible for Debbie's anguish, she had forgiven him for his little prank. Chuck was cuddling the now calm Debbie and Tristan and Aaron were helping themselves to more food and wine.

Picture perfect.

"Look I'm off, I'd better get my report done and circulate the description of our suspect," Thomas sounded as dejected as he looked.

Dan tore himself away from Tina, "Why go, there's plenty of food and booze and I'll bet matey is halfway back to Arab land by now, what's the rush?" Dan had a point, but Thomas had a full uniform on and a panda car to get back to the station. "No, thanks anyway but I'll have to get back." With that, Thomas left.

Dan went back to what was left of his barbeque, Chuck and Debbie had excused themselves and headed back to their RV to recover from the day's events. Tina, still in awe of her man, laid back on her sunbed and tried to forget the earlier phone conversation with her mother. She couldn't help but wonder what the evil-looking snake was and if Dan was involved where he was keeping it.

The remainder of the day was uneventful. People went about their way, chatting, walking, wasting time or just watching the world go by.

Chapter 14: She's Not Having It

Dan rose at his usual early hour. For a man that did bugger, all he was always up and at the office well before 7 am. No one questioned why, as all he appeared to do was sit in his office and smoke. There wasn't any actual work being done unless it was looking online for cheap caravans or cars that he could buy to resell.

Today there was nothing that caught his eye, so he sat back and lit yet another cigarette and poured his third coffee. "Ranger 1, Ranger 1, come in Ranger 1, over." It was Bob, one of the wardens Dan had inherited when he bought the site. Dan looked at the walkie-talkie and cursed wondering how he had been persuaded to these infernal bloody radios. Reluctantly he picked up his handset, "What the fuck is it, what do you bloody want, Bob?" Being disturbed this early irritated Dan, but there again being contacted by Bob at any time of the day irritated him.

"Sorry, boss, Ranger 2 here, I say Ranger 2 here, over." Dan's temper was rising; he looked in anger at the handset, "Look shit for brains you called me, so it can't be over, can it, fucking over, shithead, get the fuck on with it, what do you bloody well want?"

Bob, unperturbed at Dan's harsh response continued, "Spot of bother on the tent field, reports of possible child abuse, assistance required, I say possible child abuse in progress on the tent field, over."

Dan stared at the handset in bewilderment and disbelief. What was this idiot talking about? He grabbed the handset, "If this is a bloody joke, you and Maud are history, understand, history, what do you mean possible child abuse in progress?" Dan's patience was finished.

"Ranger 2 here, Ranger 2 here." Dan now at the point of exploding snapped back cutting Bob off, "Right shithead, I'm coming over, exactly where on the tent field are you, and if you start that Ranger fucking 2 stuff again, I won't be responsible for my actions." Bob could feel by the tone of Dan's voice that he'd better cut to the chase, "At the back by Top Field, over."

Dan didn't respond as he was already well on the way. Seeing Bob, he pulled up sharply and got out of his truck and stomped up to Bob, who gestured to Dan to be quiet by holding an index finger to his pursed lips. "Listen."

They could hear a child, a little girl by the sound of it, crying loudly and a woman's voice, an older woman's voice.

"I'm not having it, do you hear, I'm not having it, no, stop it, I'm not having it, no I'm not. I'm not having it, stop it because I'm not having it, no, not today I'm not having it, did you hear what I said, I'm not having it." Dan looked at Bob, they both stood looking puzzled. What wasn't she having, the more the woman told the child she wasn't having it, the more the child cried.

What should they do, the woman continued to repeat herself over and over.

"No, young lady, I'm not having it, no, stop that silly crying because I'm not having it, no, you can do that all day for all I care because I'm not having it." The child cried, almost building to a frenzy. The woman continued and just as Dan thought it was time to intervene a man's voice joined in.

"Now stop it, your nan's not having it, do you hear, she's not having it." His thick West Country accent and deep voice continued, "Now stop, we're not having it."

Now neither of them aren't having whatever it was they weren't having.

The man's voice continued to repeat, I'm not having it or we're not having it. It didn't make any sense. Dan turned to Bob, "I'm going to have to put a stop to this, they're waking everyone up." By now the 'I'm not or we're not having it' had been going on for over ten minutes and people were beginning to rise to see what was going on. Dan stepped forward to bang on the side of the tent.

"I'm not having it, no stop it, your nan bought you a pretty dress to wear today, so you can't put those shorts on, I don't care if you want to go to the beach, we're taking you to a walk in your pretty new dress."

Now all became clear and rather than stop a child abuse case in progress Dan knocked on the tent. "Can you come out for a moment?" Dan called. An elderly man stuck out a dishevelled grey head from the tent.

"What?" He looked bluntly at Dan. "What do you want?" His head poked through the tent flap.

Dan looked back at the old man, "Can you keep it down, you're disturbing the site?" Dan thought it a reasonable request.

"Why, what's the problem?" The old man retorted. Dan breathed in deeply, it's too fucking early to get into a pointless argument with some decrepit prick.

"Look, mate, it's not seven o'clock yet and between you and your wife and that crying kid, you've woken up most of the tent field, so unless you two shut the fuck up and stop antagonising that kid, pack your shit up and piss off, is that reason enough, and by the way, I agree with the kid, a stupid pretty frock doesn't cut it on the beach, got it?" Dan favoured the direct approach; it saved a lot of unnecessary chit-chat or misunderstanding.

The old man retreated into his tent. The child's crying subsided, and peace and quiet were restored. "Thank the fuck for that," Dan heard someone mutter from a nearby tent.

Dan turned to Bob, "What are you two on today, shitters first?" With a full site, the two toilets and shower blocks on the tent field always required an early clean and again after the morning rush.

This was music to Bob's ears, cleaning for both him and Maud was an obsession, the dirtier the better. They would lose themselves in mops and buckets, bleach and Ajax powder, absolute heaven.

"And you might as well do an early rubbish bin sort out." How campers could miss three huge skips to deposit their black bin bags was always a mystery to Dan, but miss them they, irritatingly, did.

Dan went back to his truck and drove up to a point on the site from where he could see the sea. Despite his loathing of the average man, he loved this part of the country and found those locals that he did mix with occasionally agreeable enough. A far cry from Lincolnshire, it just felt different, a place where he belonged. He sat on the bonnet of his truck for a while, smoking, watching a small boat in the bay, probably crabbing, and thought how peaceful that bloke's life must be.

In fairness, Dan's life wasn't bad, as Tina had established his expectations were low, and he had no ambition. He accepted that generally life had passed him by, so the campsite was his little kingdom to do with as he liked. He didn't need to kiss anyone's arse, which suited him fine. Mornings like this morning pissed him off because it wasn't part of his grand plan. All any punter had to do was rock up, pay up, set up and shut the fuck up. What they got up to while there were here, he didn't care about as long as it didn't affect him.

The cash rolled in and largely went into his back pocket, cash was for spending and bank accounts painted too good a picture for the taxman, so were best avoided.

The radio crackled into life, "Dan it's Tina, the DiAngelos are leaving early, are you coming back?" Not so bloody likely, thought Dan. The sooner they piss off, the better; she had been a total disappointment and yesterday's fiasco had proved Dan right, the bloody Yanks couldn't win a wet farting contest, let alone a war.

"No, Tina, I'm tied up fixing a loose fencepost, give them my regards and I hope they come back soon." There wasn't any loose post, even if there was Dan wouldn't fix it. A couple of minutes later, Dan saw the RV heading down the lane and back to the main road. Dan wondered what the rest of the holiday weekend would bring not more bloody grief! Dan picked up the radio again. "Tina, Bob and Maud are doing the shitters and the bin area, can you tell those two poofs to get the fuck out of the office and get some litter picking done, it looks like being a warm one, so make sure the ice cream freezer is fully stocked and put the prices up by 25p a go." Might as well *make hay while the sun shines*, he thought. He went back to watching the little boat bobbing about.

On top of the hill, Dan could see The Seagull Pub and what looked like Chris setting out sunshades. He hadn't been to the pub in a while so thought it would make a change for him and Tina to go out this evening.

Dan got off the bonnet of his truck, time for a drive around to see what was happening on the site.

As usual, he did the residents and favoured casuals first. Francis, the St Bernard was in his usual position laying outside watching the world go by, but watching the hippy couple strangely; Dan was sure he saw Francis winking at the bloke. His owner Margaret was already sitting in a deck chair enjoying the sunshine and peace and quiet. She gave a smile and a wave as Dan drove past. Why can't they all be like her and her husband, Dan thought, no trouble, turn up at the beginning of the season and go about their time, quietly and without disturbing anyone, pay up on time and piss off at the end of the season. Dan already had his eye on brokering a profitable deal selling their caravan when the old couple died.

A few plots along was Paul's caravan, perhaps it was his mind playing tricks, but every time Dan passed Paul's van, he swore he could smell dope. He made a mental note to drop by later and have a word, what with the local plod about yesterday he could do without the Drugs Squad raiding the place as well. There was a bit of tidying up to do, it was part of the agreement that residents had to keep their plots tidy, and the grass cut. Paul always had to be reminded.

Newcomers to the site were an Eastern European couple, Slav and Irina. She worked locally, in a warehouse of sorts and he was a long-distance lorry driver. Dan liked this pair, like the Owens, they kept themselves to themselves, but he was a good source of duty-free fags and booze, and she always had a supply of fresh meat; she wasn't too bad looking either, although Dan had erred on the side of caution as Slav did have a bit of a temper and looked like he could do some damage, and why bugger up a reliable duty-free stream for the sake of a shag!

Next was a couple that Dan couldn't work out but had his suspicions. The bloke, Steve, was a car salesman, or so he said, but Dan had his doubts. His wife or at least that's what he called her, but again Dan had his doubts, came and went at odd times. The pair were on thin ice as far as Dan was concerned. Steve, was a piss head, always drunk, wandering about the site, bottle in hand, shirtless, scruffy, literally staggering drunk. While Dan was no prude, that was a line too far and jeopardised the 'family' atmosphere Dan liked to think the site exuded. The wife, he never did catch her name, but she appeared to have several, dressed a bit tarty as Tina called it, but she had the best pair of tits Dan had ever seen, huge, but firm. Dan tried to keep the couple at arm's length because they looked like liberty takers and Dan could do without anyone trying it on, as it usually involved cash, or being late with it.

Bob and Maud had their caravan in the corner, Dan couldn't work out just why this pair irritated him so much, they hadn't given him a reason to feel like this about them. They worked hard, they were never late and never took time off. You could set your clock by them. They did have annoying little habits that Dan found to be twee, niggling and petty. Like they both walked hand in hand when they went to the Staff Shower. They both wore a onesie, took foot mats to step on and no matter who finished their ablutions first, they waited for each other and walked back, hand in hand. Bob had told Dan that each night, they religiously go to bed at 10 pm, regardless of the time of year, and had a small measure of scotch. When Dan had queried how small this measure was, Bob had signalled with his index finger and thumb an amount that would hardly wet the bottom of a glass. Their pitch was perfect. On days off, they worked in their garden, hanging baskets, gnomes, and beautiful flower beds. Even Dan had to admit it was a beautiful sight.

There were a few 'weekenders' that had paid for an all-year pitch but usually only came at weekends. There were a couple of vans owned by keen sea anglers, with the sea less than a mile away, it made a perfect place to keep a caravan. Dan had let one of the blokes keep a small boat with an outboard on the site, for the usual alcoholic or tobacco consideration. These too were people he liked, no trouble, come and go as they please, bother no one and pay up on time, perfect customers.

There was one couple who rubbed him up the wrong way. She was a solicitor in some local practise, and he owned a small business, Dan didn't know or care what it was, but the bloke would bore you to death about it, given half a chance. Her, as Dan called the wife, her, Mrs Bloody Know it All, would spout the law at you if she thought that she was being unfairly dealt with over any little matter. Dan had already told Tina, that under no circumstances was she to pander to any of their frequent requests. We might be a little late on Friday, can we have the gate code so we can let ourselves in, or, we have friends coming this weekend, can they pitch their tent in front of our van?

The answer was always 'no.' That, Dan said, would never change and as soon as they stepped over the line, Dan would make sure he cancelled their seasonal agreement. They had got on Dan's wrong side shortly after Dan had bought the site by parking their car in the staff car park and when Dan asked him to move it to the resident's car park, she flatly refused saying that 'secure parking' was part of their seasonal agreement. Of course, it wasn't, but she had felt that it was in the spirit of the agreement that allowed them to do so. A copy of their agreement with the parking section highlighted in yellow was hand-delivered to their caravan with a letter stating any abuse of the arrangement would lead to the cancelling of their agreement. Since that day they hadn't spoken to Dan, which suited Dan just fine.

There were several more residents that Dan got on with, or perhaps that would be better worded as they got on with Dan.

Dan continued his round heading toward the tent fields; there were three in total with excellent facilities. The shower and toilet blocks were new when Dan bought the place and played a major part in Dan's decision in buying the site. Dan pulled up outside the biggest block to find Bob and Maud flopping the mop and generally giving the place a good going over. Dan didn't bother acknowledging either Bob or Maud and after seeing the cleaning was underway, left.

Just as he reached his truck, a couple of tents caught his attention. Due to fire risks and therefore complying with tent or caravan distance separation rules, as stipulated in his site insurance, what was strictly not allowed was tents pitching up right next to each other. The insurance also said that 'fencing, temporary or otherwise' was not allowed, in fact, anything that could be a barrier to access for Emergency Services was strictly forbidden.

In front of him, Dan was confronted by three tents all touching each other with a windbreak fence surrounding all three like a corral. Dan stood and looked at ten or twelve children of various ages running amok, while their mothers sat drinking wine and generally ignoring their offspring.

Dan went into his truck and picked up the radio. "Tina, who the fuck pitched the three tents with dozens of kids in the main field near the big block shitters?"

Tina responded, "Is there a problem, darling?"

"Only that they've set up a corral arrangement and all three tents are touching each other, so my bloody insurance is completely fucking worthless if anything happens and judging by the useless bitches these kids are with that's very likely to happen." Dan was incensed that whoever organised their pitches obviously hadn't done it properly. Although Dan would be the first to admit he did bugger all, he was serious about safety, especially if it meant ignoring it could land him in prison.

Tina came back on the radio, "Bob pitched them yesterday, shall I call him?"

Dan looked back at the shitters where Bob was, "No thanks, he's right here, I'll sort it out." With that, Dan called Bob on the radio.

"Bob, whatever you are doing stop it immediately and come outside the reception end door."

Thirty seconds later, Bob replied, "Give me ten minutes and I'll be right there."

Dan's anger reached an exploding point, "If you aren't here within thirty seconds, you and your bloody wife can pack up and fuck off, that's now twenty seconds."

The door opened and Bob appeared. "What's up, boss?" Bob looked nervously at Dan.

"That is," Dan pointed to the corral, "you're a sorry excuse for a man at the best of times, just how bloody long have you been doing this job, you know the rules and you know how much I pay to insure this bloody circus, sort this shit out and don't, and I mean don't, do fuck anything else until this is sorted out, do you bloody well understand, just nod, Bob, just nod, because if you say something stupid, you are likely to die." Dan got in his truck and pulled away.

The feeling of rage, anger and disbelief that someone with Bob's experience could ignore, or allow someone to ignore, basic safety rules was beyond him. There is a saying that goes something along the lines of that when it comes to reputation shit sticks, but as far as Dan was concerned blood stick's a bloody sight better with greater consequences. He pondered sacking Bob and kicking him and his wife off the site immediately, but that could result in the pair taking legal action and required a paper trail which Dan hadn't got. Instead, he drove back to the reception and immediately into his office. "Tina, is that bloke still on site, you know the one that's just taken a seasonal pitch, Joe I think his name is, I saw him yesterday, has he left?"

Tina looked at the register of residents who had to book in and out of the site for safety reasons, "It looks like he's still here, why has he done something?"

Dan walked out of his office and through reception towards his truck, "Don't worry, I need to ask his advice, that's all." With that, Dan headed to Joe's caravan.

Of all the people Dan had met since buying the site, Joe and his wife Linda, he had taken an immediate liking to. Joe was a director of some big company and Linda was a senior manager of an international firm with offices in the city. What attracted Dan was the plain-speaking that both Joe and Linda did, and their complete openness and honesty. That coupled with their sense of fun and the occasional spontaneous barbeque and drinking session which followed, just made them fun to be around.

Although Joe was highly approachable, Dan was cautious around him. Joe exuded a presence, a no-nonsense, hard, almost frightening air that unnerved people. If he asked a question of someone, he seemed to fix them with a stare that was like them being trapped in a car's headlights. He had that knack of staying quiet for a few seconds longer when he was given an answer as if doubting what he had been told. As Dan knew all too well, there are hard men and there are hard men. You don't have to be physically violent to be a hard man, and as far as Dan was concerned, Joe was a hard man.

Arriving at their caravan, Dan could see the pair in their garden, Joe as usual sprawled out on a sunbed in his speedo's soaking up the sun.

Joe could always be found on his sunbed, it's my way of doing sod all and unwinding, he told Dan. Dan exited his truck and lit a cigarette, "Joe, Linda, sorry to bother you but could I ask your advice?" Dan went on to explain that he should have had certain policies in place by now but had been a bit tardy in getting them done, but now it was apparent that he needed to do it. What Dan needed was a bit of a shopping list, to say the least, Health & Safety, Equal Opportunities, HR, the list was endless.

Joe discussed each in detail and how best to approach it, after all, he had years of experience in writing and implementing every policy or procedure Dan required. "Can you write these for me?" Or is there anywhere Dan could buy them, he asked. Joe, in his usual pragmatic way, explained the process and how most H&S policies were an adaptation of someone else's. Joe said that he'd get all the policies Dan required and next weekend, they could go through each and adjust them to suit the site, but he made Dan aware that merely lining up an impressive array of policies on a shelf and ignoring implementing them was worse than not having any in the first place. Dan looked confused but happy that his newfound friend was willing to help.

At last, the day was improving, or so Dan thought.

Chapter 15: Weekend Guests

As with most weekends, holidaymakers that were there for a week or two usually had visitors, family or friends wanting to come and share a few hours together. As far as Dan was concerned that was ok on two provisos. The first being they contributed to the 'Flower Fund,' which could be loosely interpreted as Dan's Booze and Fag Fund, and the second being that they behaved and fucked off by 6 pm.

Most visitors accepted this.

Mid-morning saw Dan in his office with Tina going through the numbers for the weekend. By any measure, the takings were up and buoyed up further with extortionately priced groceries and ice creams. Dan watched the steady flow of visitors popping into the office to 'contribute.'

Three large estate cars with Lithuanian number plates pulled up which contained several burly men and several impossibly horny girls. Dan's attention went immediately, from matters fiscal to matters frisky. Tina looked worried, after the Debbie DiAngelo fiasco the last thing she needed was another interruption to Dan's libido. Dan, aware of Tina's unease made a passing comment, "Oh, look at this lot, they can fuck off as soon as they like." This did nothing to reassure Tina.

The reception door swung open and a man in a tight t-shirt with a bodybuilder's physique and chiselled facial features stood in the doorway with a couple of cases of strong Lithuanian lager in his arms. "Dan?" The man looked at Dan quizzically, "You Dan?" Dan looked at him hoping that these were friends of Slav and Irina.

"Yes, mate, that's me." Placing the two cases of lager on the desk the man grinned, "Slav, my friend, he comes now," his thick Eastern European accent echoed around the room, "he tells me for you," the man pointed towards the cases of booze. "There is more in the car and smokes." With that, he left the reception and gestured to the others to fetch the rest of the 'duty-free.' Normally, Dan welcomed the arrangement, but he had an uneasy feeling about today.

The car's occupants stretched in the warm sunlight and looked around at the surroundings. Two more men appeared at the reception, each placing more cases of lager, vodka and boxes of cigarettes on the desk. A couple of shoppers were looking at the transaction suspiciously. Dan seeing their interest started picking up the boxes and nodding to the others to bring all the 'duty-free' into the back office. "Of course, we can look after these for you two gentlemen," Dan said hoping this would avert the shopper's attention.

Not understanding Dan's comment, chiselled features said, "No, Slav say for you, take much booze and fags for my friend Dan, you keep."

Dan winced, "Oh, do thank Slav for me." The man looked at Dan, "No need to thank Slav, he likes you to have." Now was the time for this lot to bugger off before somebody reports this to plod.

Out of the window, Dan spotted Irina talking to the gathering. Seeing Dan, Irina came into the office. "Tina, I'm sorry, I should have told you sooner about Slav's brother and some of his cousins coming today, is ok with you?"

Tina looked at Dan, "Of course, it is Irina, they're here just for the day, aren't they? Do remember the 6 pm deadline, otherwise, we might get complaints from other campers." Irina nodded and along with her guests made their way to their caravan.

Tina looked at Dan, "I hope that doesn't get out of hand as they look like they could get a bit rowdy with a couple of drinks inside of them."

Dan nodded, "Don't worry, Slav, won't screw up things here, it's too good a place for them."

At Slav and Irina's van, Slav had already filled a dustbin with ice and crammed as many bottles as possible of Svyturys Ekstra beer into it. He filled another with Stolichnaya vodka. A selection of cold meats along with several loaves of bread were arranged on a table. The scene was set for a traditional Lithuanian gathering. Slav and Irina greeted their guests with warm hugs and strong drinks. It didn't take long before the noise level increased and continued to rise with each round of drinks.

Even from the reception Dan and Tina could hear laughter and cheer, *why are they bloody cheering?* Dan thought. Aaron wandered into the office, "I've had people complaining about that Russian bloke and his bird, they say the noise is deafening and they've started singing shouty songs." Dan feared that might be the case, but not this soon, it wasn't even mid-day yet. He looked at Aaron's pale features and thought about sending him to ask Slav and company to tone it down a bit, but if Aaron referred to Slav as Russian the chances of him seeing the rest of the day out were slim to non-existent. Tina got up from her chair, "Won't be a minute," she said as she walked outside and lit a cigarette. Dan sat at his desk tapping a pen on a coffee mug wondering if he should intervene sooner rather than later with Slav's gathering.

Tina cut across the field and into the resident's area heading towards Slav's caravan. Even at a distance, she could see dancing and hear singing, Slav appeared to be the leading voice in The Flying Hussar, a traditional folk song, that his guests joined in raucously at every chorus. "Tina, so glad you come, please sit here," Irina enthused and thrust a large glass of Stolichnaya into her hand. Tina was not expecting such a warm response and was immediately caught up in the alcoholic merriment. "Come, come, Tina, please, dance," Slav pulled Tina to her feet and swept her into the centre of the throng throwing her side to side enthusiastically. Round and around, she went enthralled in a world of Lithuanian culture and strong drink. "Irina, please, Tina needs another drink, please our guest." Slav twirled Tina around, releasing her next to the drinks table. Another Stolichnaya was swiftly followed by another and another and soon Tina's inhibitions, well what she had left of them, were lost. Unbuttoning her top to reveal more of her ample breasts, she twirled and bumped. Her breasts threatening to break free of their fetters at any moment, she twerked her bum enticingly at Karolis, Slav's cousin. The music played, the booze flowed, and Tina danced with gay abandon.

Dan decided that he couldn't leave it any longer and headed to Slav's caravan. If he got in now perhaps, he could persuade Slav to take his guests elsewhere before things got any louder. Dan stopped short, was that Tina dancing with her tits almost hanging out? Why the fuck was she rubbing her fanny up against the big fucker that had been in reception earlier, no hang on she was rubbing up against that greasy-looking prick, who by the look on his face wanted to do more than dance. "Shit, this is all I fucking need, her pissed and the object of Baltic Lothario." This is going to get messy.

Dan did his best to approach without being seen, if only he could catch her attention perhaps, he could get her to leave the party before things got any worse.

The plan failed miserably.

On seeing Dan waving frantically for her to move away, Tina shouted, "Oh look, Slav, Dan has come to join us." She twirled away again, a little more unsteadily than before.

Dan stood up. "Well, that's thrown a fucking Baltic-sized fucking hammer in my fucking plan," and with that, Dan had little choice but to join the gathering. Slav and Irina's welcome was overwhelming and with the usual Lithuanian enthusiasm, everyone was soon hugging and kissing him. "Beer, my friend, beer." Slav insisted Dan partake. Dan, for once in his life didn't want to drink, but accepted the cold beer and made his way through the dancing Tina.

He caught her arm and tried to stop her twirling and twerking before Karolis took her from behind. "Tina," he hissed through gritted teeth, "what the hell are you doing?" His question went unanswered. "Tina, for heaven's sake, stop acting like a slapper and pull yourself together." She still didn't answer. Karolis seemed intent on taking her there and then. Dan stood in between them, "Oi Stavros, do yourself a favour and fuck off." Dan's message was clear, and although very drunk Karolis could see the afternoon's intended fun with Tina wasn't going to happen if Dan had anything to do with it.

"Come on, baby, dance with me." Tina threw her arms drunkenly around Dan's neck. "Dance fucking dance, with you! Flinging your arse about the place like a bitch on heat, like some slapper off Union Street?"

Dan was done with reasoning; the gathering was beginning to get way too far out of hand and too damn quickly.

"Danny, Danny, you come dance with me." Dan swung around to see a tall striking blonde with little tits, but big nipples, poking out from under a tight pink tee-shirt, why do I always see the tits first, Dan thought. "Come on, Danny, dance," This was going from bad to worse. Dan pulled back, as nice as it would be to get up close and personal with this horny Eastern European beauty, he feared it would soon turn into a Euro-Wife-Swop of epic proportions and he wasn't prepared to stir anyone's porridge.

There was nothing for it.

Dan tugged at Slav's arm, interrupting the final verse of some other deeply nostalgic folk song. "Slav, I've had the cops on the phone, they say they're coming over to investigate some illegally imported booze, I think someone shopped your mates bringing the stuff into reception." Slav stopped singing, wiping tears of nostalgia from his eyes he looked at Dan. "Cops, come here, for booze and smokes?" Slav had got the message. What he didn't need was Customs and Excise raiding the place and ruining a perfectly organised smuggling ring. "Dan, I go, take all stuff with me and hide in lock-up, yes."

Dan nodded, "And quickly, get the stuff out of my office as well."

Slav understood perfectly and issued hurried Lithuanian instructions to the gathering to load the cars and piss off. Well, that's what Dan assumed he had said as everyone and everything, was gone in five minutes.

Turning to Tina, he glared at her, what a bloody fine display she had made of herself. Tina was past caring, all that vodka and dancing had left her exhausted and as far as she was concerned, Dan was getting a taste of his own medicine, although she doubted, he was Karolis's type.

As far as Dan was concerned, that bloody debacle was an experience he'd rather not repeat and would have to review the visitor's policy. He also needed to be more discreet with the flow of duty-free contraband that came on-site. Bundling an inebriated Tina into his truck he had no choice but to take her home to sleep off the morning's excesses. "Are you coming to join me in bed, honey?" Tina patted the end of the bed provocatively, looking at Dan.

Dan grimaced at the thought and sighed, "Not so bloody likely, the way my day's going, you'll puke all over me, go to bloody sleep."

Dan's usual day of doing bugger all wasn't working out.

Chapter 16: Roxy

Dan's day continued to stumble along. The shop was busy and as Tina was otherwise incapacitated, it was down to him to staff the shop and the office, a job he loathed with a passion.

"Have you got any bubble gum, mister?" The detestable ginger child from yesterday stood in front of the sweet rack. "If I've got it, it'll be there," Dan said without acknowledging the child.

"I mean the big pink ones; we get them at home, don't you have them here in this shitty shop?" Dan looked at the child, why did ginger kids always look so bloody ugly?

"Oi, ginger, before I lose my temper, why don't you bugger off?"

Ginger remembered Dan's reaction from yesterday. "But I want the pink bubble gum, like the stuff I get at home, why don't you have it, grumpy guts?"

Dan looked down at the child, "Are you with that group of tents near the big shower block?"

The child stared back at Dan and pointed towards the door, "Over there you mean, near that big place where people go with towels, where my mum took my little brother when he shit himself?" There was no doubting the child's logic, no matter how distastefully it was put.

"Yes, that bunch," Dan replied.

"My mum said that other old man was a prick and that he could go and fuck himself, my aunty said that they would put up the tents how they fucking like and they told him to fuck off."

Dan had heard enough, "Shops shut. So, bugger off," and again he marshalled ginger out the door." Had Bob sorted out the problem like Dan had told him? He'd better check.

Getting into his truck, he radioed Bob, "Did you sort out those tents I told you about this morning?" Bob confirmed he had, although the two mothers were annoyed that he wanted their little encampment pulling down. "Did you actually see them move the fence and move the tents?" It was like drawing teeth.

"Well, no, I asked them to do it and they said they would."

Dan leant on the steering wheel, "So you didn't see it done, but you've checked it since to make sure?" The radio stayed silent, "Bob, I take it from your lack of response you haven't."

The radio crackled, "Not yet, I was just going to when you called me." Bob was a dreadful liar.

Dan decided that he'd leave it to Bob to check as quite frankly, he was fed up with the way Bob had handled things. He really needed Joe and Linda to come up with those policies so he could build the paper trail he needed to get rid of Bob and Maud. Roll on the weekend, for a man that detested bureaucracy, in all its forms, having the right policies behind him at last, could only be a plus.

With that, he decided tonight he'd eat at the pub and leave Tina to sleep.

As soon as he'd closed the office, Dan jumped in his truck and headed for The Seagull. He liked the pub and Chris; they held a similar outlook on life. Dan entered the bar and exchanged the usual niceties with Chris. He sat at the bar enjoying the peace and quiet and a few moments of solitude. His solitude was short-lived. "Evening, Dan." Dan heard Paul's voice, "Can I get you one?" Paul said knowing Dan had just got a drink. Dan wondered if he could get away with ignoring him.

Chris appeared out of nowhere, "That's good of Paul, I'll put it in, shall I, Dan?" Dan looked at Chris who winked as he held out his hand for the money, which Paul dug into his pockets for.

"That's funny, I could have sworn I had a tenner on me." Paul searched his pockets while Chris left his hand out. "Bless me, I seem to have lost it, can you put it on my tab please?" Chris looked at Paul in disbelief, "What tab, since when did you have a tab here and you bloody well know it, pay up."

With that, Paul produced a ten-pound note. "Dan, could I talk to you in private in the back room?" Chris gestured to the pool table in the back room while giving Paul his change. Dan followed Chris, "What's up?" Dan asked.

"Nothing, I just wanted that prick to piss off; I'm sick of him taking advantage with that short arms and deep pocket routine, he took advantage of a couple in here yesterday." The pair went back into the bar, Paul had left feeling hurt that he hadn't managed to con yet another free drink out of someone.

Chris went back to serving and Dan continued in his solitude.

Dan daydreamed, not about anything, but let his mind wander. He was looking at the back of a woman in a leopard skin pattern dress, a bit tight fitting for a woman of generous, but in proportion figure. Her blonde hair was perfectly groomed. The bloke she was with Dan didn't recognise, but why would he, this was a holiday weekend so there were plenty of strangers about, but there was something familiar about her that Dan couldn't quite put his finger on. He racked his brains trying to think where he had heard that voice before. After five minutes Dan shrugged, sod it, it's not important and he finished his pint and waited for Chris to refill his glass.

"Anyone using this chair?" It was the bloke from the end of the bar. Dan looked up, "No, help yourself." With that, the bloke picked up the chair and placed it so that the leopard skin dress woman could be seated. Now she was sitting looking directly in Dan's direction. Dan couldn't believe who he was looking at, piss-head Steve's wife, no doubt about it. The hair was a different colour, but those huge firm tits were hers. The makeup was a bit heavy, a bit tarty, but there was probably a good reason for that.

She looked at Dan and smiled.

Yes, it was, her. Her low-cut dress revealed more of her huge breasts, which pushed forward as she seated herself on the chair.

Dan turned to Chris, "Does she come in a lot?" He asked. Chris didn't have to look to know who Dan meant.

"Roxy?" Chris replied. Dan looked puzzled.

"Roxy, is that her name?"

"Well, you should know, doesn't she live on your site?" Well, if it was her, and Dan was sure it was, he sure as hell didn't know her name was Roxy. Chris leant forward so as not to be overheard, "You know, she's on the game, don't you? Different bloke every night, you must have seen her ad in the personal columns of the Argus."

Now Dan was puzzled, no he didn't read a local paper and if he did, he never read the personal columns, picking up a bird there would be like shitting on your own doorstep. Dan was sure Chris had got it wrong, he had to be, but it would explain the comings and goings at all hours. "She's married, her husband is that piss-head I keep meaning to get rid of."

Chris chuckled, "Doesn't mean you can't earn a bit on the side, or on your back, does it?"

Dan would have to have a word with Tina. What with a drunken Lithuanian nostalgia fest, a madman blowing up things and now Roxy Piss-head on the game; his site was deteriorating before his eyes.

Things had to change.

Chapter 17: Bob's Last Stand

Bob made his way to the illegally erected corral. He didn't do confrontation, especially with two single, loudmouthed women from Essex. He approached cautiously hoping that the offending fence would have been taken down and the tents moved.

No such luck.

Fence and tents remained illegally erected.

There was nothing for it, either face Dan's rage or face two tarts from Essex. The lesser of the two evils being the tarts. He was almost at the tents when a voice from inside stopped him in his tracks.

"Oh, for fucks sake, he's pissed the bed, I can't believe it, the dirty little fucker has pissed himself, this is all I fucking need, a couple of days away and this little shit can't control himself and pisses the bed." As she vented her anger, the higher and shriller her voice became. "I guess I should be grateful you didn't shit yourself, but for fucks sake, why didn't you go before you went to bed?"

Bob guessed that perhaps can after can of fizzy drinks all day long had a lot to do with it.

"Get the fuck up, come on, get up, how the fuck you expect me to get this dry, fuck only knows."

Bob hesitated a little longer.

As he stood hesitating to the point of almost retreating, a tent flap opened. An angry woman exited carrying a wet sleeping bag and blanket. She looked at Bob, Bob looked at her. The look in her eyes was far more determined than Bob's. "And what the fuck do you want again?" She had come out fighting.

Bob swallowed heavily and cleared his throat. "You were told this morning that you had to move the tents at least three metres apart and that fence of windbreaks had to go, why hasn't it?" Bob was pleased with his authoritative tone. She was in no mood to be told what to do by Bob or anyone else,

"Why don't you go and fuck yourself, just who the fuck do you think you are telling me what to do?" Bob looked shocked at her hostile response.

"You were told when you arrived that for safety reasons the tents had to be…" The angry Essex woman cut Bob short, "Oh fuck off, nothing better to do but harass a defenceless woman, such a man aren't you, piss off for fuck's sake before I give you a slap." Bob was losing this argument big time. He stepped closer to the illegal settlement, he had to enforce his authority, although the defenceless women comment had unsettled him. "You simply can't, under any circumstances, have tents erected so close to each other, I must insist."

Essex woman moved closer, "I bet that's the only time you get an erection," she sneered, "when you're putting up a tent."

Essex woman 1 was joined by Essex woman 2, "Go on, Laura, tell the perv to fuck off, I bet he was coming to steal some of your panties." The pair shrieked with laughter. Bob stood quietly, disarmed by their crude comments. It was no good, he couldn't do confrontation, it just wasn't in his nature.

He'd failed, again and this time, it could mean getting fired; after all these happy years, gone because of these two tarts.

He turned to walk away in shame.

"Right, let's be having you." Bob turned to look back. There was Maud like he'd never seen her, tearing into the windbreak corral, throwing them in a heap. She turned to the tents, kicking out the ground pegs causing both tents to fall limp.

"Right," she hissed, "you've been told time and time again to shift these bloody things and done nothing, well I'm here to help you, got it." The two Essex women looked at Maud, taken aback at her forthright, no-nonsense approach. Maud rounded on the one with the foul mouth, "You, get this crap picked up and throw it in your car, you're not leaving piss-soaked bedding all over the place, other people don't want to see it."

With that Essex woman 1 complied, not daring to anger Maud further.

"My husband tried and bloody tried, but you couldn't do it when he asked nicely, so now, you have me to answer to, shift it, now."

Bob, stood in amazement as Maud forced the pair into action. At just 5' 4" tall and just over six stone in weight, Maud was a powerhouse, not taking no for an answer, she was in control, not two gobby Essex tarts. What he had dreaded all day and achieved nothing; Maud had done in minutes.

She turned to Bob, "Go and put the kettle on, Bob, there's a love, I won't be a minute," Maud smiled and Bob, being the dutiful husband, left to put the kettle on. Twenty-three years of married life and he'd never seen Maud raise her voice.

Fifteen minutes later, Maud now stood in the re-organised pitch, the tents separated, the corral gone. Essex women defeated. Maud turned to the two women, "Don't let me be forced to come back here again, I won't be so lenient a second time."

Essex women nodded.

Maud left.

Chapter 18: All Tits and Teeth

Dan had finished his pint and was feeling decidedly uneasy about Roxy Piss Head and her nefarious activity. He hoped he was wrong but, after what Chris had said and her strange comings and goings, the evidence, if you could call it evidence, did seem to bare out his supposition.

"Another," Chris pointed to Dan's empty glass. "No, I'd better not, I should get back, we've got a strange bunch in this weekend and with Tina in bed with a hangover, I'd better go." Dan stood up, shook hands with Chris and headed for the door. "See you later, Danny," Roxy Piss Head called out to him.

Dan turned, half smiling, and he nodded. "I knew those two fuckers were going to be trouble," he muttered as he closed the door behind him.

During the short drive down the hill and back to the site, Dan thought about Roxy Piss Head, she wasn't a bad looker, huge tits, and a bit on the plump side, but she looked in proportion, nice teeth, why did he notice tits first and teeth second, fuck knows! Was she flogging it, did her piss-head husband know, did he care, how long has she been at it, where does she get at it, she threw up more questions than answers. Should he tell Tina, or just confront Roxy or whatever she would be called tomorrow? Fuck me, what a bloody weekend this was turning into.

Dan pulled into the site. All seemed ok, smoke from dozens of barbeques hung in the air and there was a gentle hum of people chatting, sitting about and enjoying the evening setting sun. The daytime noise from children playing had died down and now it was the adults' time to relax. Dan loved this time of day.

He tried to resist the urge to drive around the site, but just as his early morning round had become a ritual, so was his evening round. He decided to start at the far end and drive back, checking that those bloody throw-away barbeques that had become so popular weren't too close to anything that could catch fire. He hated the damn things, they were an accident waiting to happen, a barbeque is usually accompanied by alcohol of some type, alcohol reduces responsibility and common sense, fire spreads, and tents are flammable, so hey, presto you've got the perfect mix for a bloody disaster. On reaching the Essex woman's tents, he paused.

Well, fuck me, Bob had done what he was told and got those two tarts to sort their shit out, Dan thought. He sat for a moment looking at the re-arranged tents. Nothing more to see or say about it, he thought, and decided to check that the showers and toilets had been done, most people had finished with them by now. He walked in one door, through the length of the showers, pushed each trap door open, flushed each toilet and headed out the other door. Perfect.

"Oi, you, get the fuck up and go for a piss." Essex woman had stirred. "Come on, get the fuck up, you heard me, I'm not going through all the shit again, that fucking warden will kick us the fuck off if she comes back, come on, do you hear me, get up and go for a piss, while you're at it, try having a crap as well, I don't want bloody disturbing again." Essex woman was thinking ahead.

Dan sat back in the comfort of his truck and wondered how some of these kids survive, it wasn't because of their parents, but despite them.

He sat a few minutes longer as the ginger kid emerged from a tent and went into the toilets.

"Grumpy guts," the ginger kid said as he passed Dan.

"Coppertop," Dan responded, too tired now to bother insulting the little shit any further.

Dan decided enough was enough, and that bottle of Irish Whiskey beckoned.

Chapter 19: A Nice Little Earner

Following an uneventful, peaceful night, Dan was up and going about his usual routines. He sat in his office enjoying endless mugs of coffee and cigarettes and pondered on yesterday's issues and how he was going to deal with them. Roxy's was a bit delicate as he didn't have hard evidence that she was 'doing it' on his site, but that threw up the question if she wasn't 'entertaining' here, where was she doing it?

He also needed to speak to Slav, yesterday's gathering was too much, as was the flow of contraband. He also had to get to the bottom of what Slav had meant when he said, 'all stuff'; just how much 'stuff' did he have on the site. Defrauding HMRC of a bit of tax was one thing, grand larceny on an industrial scale was entirely different, which carried a custodial sentence, meaning the close confines with hundreds of sex-starved men and everyone taking it up the tail, which Dan was in no hurry to try.

He shuddered at the thought and lit another cigarette.

Better get to Slav first.

Slav, like Dan, was an early riser and Dan found him clearing away the empty bottles and uneaten food outside his caravan and looking unaffected considering the amount of booze he and his cousins shifted yesterday. Slav must have been expecting Dan as he moved to greet him. Holding out his arms to welcome him, he said, "Dan, my friend, sorry, what can I say, I mean you no disrespect, my family I tell, no more, Dan is my friend." Dan was grateful that Slav was taking this conciliatory approach.

Dan moved closer to Slav so as not to be overheard. "Slav, yesterday you said 'all' that stuff, what exactly do you mean by 'all'?"

Slav looked around, sharing Dan's concern for confidentiality. "Dan, I have some of the stuff here, so that I can get it quickly for sell." This revelation didn't give Dan the answer he wanted.

Dan pressed Slav further, "I need to know how much 'Stuff' is here on my site, a couple of cases, ten cases, more?"

Slav could see Dan was worried. Slav looked around again checking to see if no one was in earshot. "Maybe two-hundred cases of vodka, a few beers and fifty, maybe more smokes." Slav beckoned to Dan to follow him into the large awning attached to his caravan. Pulling back some ornate curtains, Slav revealed the extent of his contraband enterprise.

Dan felt sick.

He had to tell Slav to get the 'stuff' off the site and quickly, but how could he do it without offending what he could now see was a serious gangster?

"Slav, what are you doing to me, this is a holiday park in East Sussex, and I can't have all of that here, surely you know we get all sorts of people coming through here, it's ok for you if the site gets raided, you can fuck off back to Lithuania, I'll be doing a 10-stretch in the Scrubs." It could have been worded a little better, but nerves were getting the better of Dan.

Slav rubbed his chin showing off his enormous biceps. "I talk to Uncle Albertas, today, he's boss, and he tells me what to do." Dan looked at the ground, now feeling ten times worse than he had before, Uncle Albertas, who the fuck was Uncle Albertas? His mind now conjured up images of Marlon Brando in *The Godfather*. What the fuck had he let happen?

Dan's problem was that he thought of himself as a bit of a shady character, part of the crew, respected, even feared. He wasn't. The people he mixed with, who might be on the far edges of criminality, were just little people feeding off the scraps of the people far down the food chain from the big boys at the top. There was the odd bit of muscle that mixed with lower ranks, topping up their earnings with a bit of protection here and there, but were by and large just little league.

Now with reality setting in, Dan needed a bloody good plan before Uncle Albertas took over everything Dan had worked for. "Look, Slav, I'm the boss around here, and I'm telling you to get the 'stuff' off the site and bloody quick. I've had the police sniffing about and it's only a question of time before they put two and two together and raid your place, do you understand?" Of course, Slav did, he knew that eventually, all safe places become unsafe, but Slav was not the boss, Uncle Albertas was, and Slav wasn't about to cross him.

Slav had taken a stance that Dan had never seen before. He wasn't listening and Dan needed to impress upon him the situation he was in. "Look, Slav, speak to this uncle of yours and tell him the 'stuff' must go, and I mean today."

Slav nodded, "I set up a meeting with uncle and you, today, yes?"

Dan looked startled, "No, don't set up a meeting, I don't need a meeting with your bloody uncle, just tell him to get the bloody stuff off my site, today, this morning, if not sooner, and no more 'stuff' here."

Dan retreated to his truck; he needed time to think. Dan pulled up at his quiet spot and leant back on the bonnet of his truck. The pleasant rolling hills of East Sussex had taken on the air of rural Sicily or whatever the Lithuanian equivalent was. He couldn't think straight. He needed to confide in someone, and Chris was his best bet, not part of the site and he probably didn't know the faces involved.

Although still early, he knew Chris would be up and about.

Dan knocked gently on the pub's kitchen door, although it was open, Dan didn't like to just walk in. Chris appeared holding a mug of coffee, surprised to see Dan again so soon and so early.

The look on Dan's face was solemn, concerned, and possibly frightened. "Problems, mate?" Chris asked. Dan told Chris the whole story leaving out anything that might incriminate him. Chris listened without interrupting. He sat quietly for a minute or so after Dan had finished telling all.

"Well, mate, you certainly do have a problem, come with me." Chris led Dan into his stockroom, he pulled a few cases of regular stock forward to reveal about 20 cases of vodka, beer, various other well-known spirits and several cases of branded cigarettes. "Oh, for fuck's sake, not you as well?" Dan's heart sank.

Chris looked hard at Dan, "Oh, come on, Dan, you must have known that Slav was selling this stuff off your site, I get this off him so cheap I can't turn it down, and the fags are a fraction of the wholesaler's price, it's a nice little earner, you sell the fags and booze, don't you?"

No, he didn't, anything he got from Slav was for his consumption only.

Things couldn't get any worse or could they?

His idyllic life was taking on a sinister undertone that he didn't like.

He just wanted to go back to perving on birds with great tits, drinking too much, taking photos of his cock, sexting with the odd bird and doing sod all, what was wrong with that. Putting his hand on Dan's shoulder, Chris looked at Dan, "Look, mate, don't start panicking, you've been getting Slav's stuff for months, nothing has happened, so why start rocking the boat now, everyone's earning out of it and even if something did happen, I think Slav's uncle has enough high-rank old bill in his pocket nothing would happen to the likes of us."

This wasn't any consolation, although Chris did have a point. He could turn a blind eye, but what if they started leaning on him to have more 'family' move onto the site? After chatting a bit more, Dan excused himself and drove back to the site.

He wondered if he was being stupid, why wouldn't Slav approach Chris, it was an outlet on the doorstep, why would Chris refuse such an easy earner, was he panicking unnecessarily?

It was one thing after another.

Chapter 20: Indecent Proposal

The site was coming to life, with campers milling about. Those that were only there for the long weekend were starting to pack up ready for the off. The lucky ones, that had booked a longer stay, idled about watching the less fortunate pack up to piss off.

Tina was already in the office, feeling guilty about yesterday and getting pissed leaving Dan to do all the work. Dan walked in, "How are you feeling, hangover?"

Tina looked at him. "Sorry about that, I got caught up in the moment, the music, the dancing, the vodka, I wasn't expecting to…"

Dan's expression made her stop mid-sentence, "Expecting what, to nearly get shagged by the Lithuanian mafia, get caught up in the biggest smuggling ring on the South Coast, land me in the biggest heap of shit there is, lose every fucking thing I've worked for, send me to the shovel for a 10-stretch, lose my bum virginity?"

Tina stood open-mouthed. "I only got a bit tipsy, that's all, what are you on about, where did you sleep last night, why the sudden interest in losing your anal virginity, what are you trying to tell me, did 'something' happen last night?" Dan wasn't making any sense.

"Sleep! Bloody sleep, I'll be lucky if I ever sleep again, what with crazed terrorists, the fucking mafia, Roxy flogging it, those halfwits you call employees doing half a fucking job, and no nothing 'happened' last night, not like that." Dan slumped in his chair.

"Whatever is wrong with you, whatever bed you got out of, it was the wrong side." Tina turned her back on him and made some coffee. "How about I get Maud to man the office and you can tell me what this is about."

Dan's head spun around, "No not that, for fucks sake, keep her out of the bloody office, and another thing, no booze, no fags, nothing dodgy is to come in here, ever, right."

He closed the door and beckoned Tina closer, "Did you know Slav was storing loads of booze and fags in his awning?" By Tina's shocked look, it was obvious she didn't,

"Ok, did you know the piss-head wife is flogging it?"

Tina frowned "Flogging what, Slav's booze and fags?"

Dan put his head in his hands, "No, you silly daft slapper, her fanny, she's flogging her fanny." Tina had horrible visions of Roxy carrying out self-flagellation beating her lady parts,

"Flogging?" Tina made hand movements like she was hitting something.

"Oh, for the life of me, Tina, sometimes I think you aren't just acting at being a complete fucking airhead, no I don't mean beating the shit out of her fanny, I mean selling it, you know tenner a shag or whatever." Tina stirred her coffee.

"Well, a tenner's not much, I wouldn't do it for less than twenty, well if it was a slow day maybe fifteen, depends I suppose on who it is." She looked thoughtful. Dan looked disgusted. Tina looked up deep in thought.

"So, all those blokes that kept coming to see Roxy, weren't part of her Bible class?" The only missionary position Roxy was thinking of taking up wasn't in the deepest Africa!

Dan stared at Tina, "What the hell are you thinking about?" He shook his head in disbelief at what he was hearing.

Tina looked up, "Oh there was a message from her for you, she wants to see you."

Amazed and slightly perturbed at Tina's line of thought, he left the office. Time to confront Roxy, or whoever she was today. He pulled up at the entrance to the resident's field, Steve Piss-Head's car was gone, he decided to be discreet and walked to their caravan so as not to draw attention to himself.

He opened the awning, no sign of life, perhaps they both went out. Cautiously he knocked on the door. "Hi, good morning, anyone home, coooeee." He heard movement from within the caravan. "It's Dan, the site owner, you wanted to see me, actually I need to see you."

"Oh, just a moment, I'm just getting ready." It was obviously Roxy in the caravan, and he'd only just caught her before she went out. A few minutes passed. "Ok, you can come in now." Come in! Dan was expecting her to come out, but what the fuck, what he had to say it was probably better done in private. Dan opened the caravan door; inside was dimly lit and the smell of very strong perfume made him cough a little.

He looked around, Roxy wasn't in the lounge area, he looked up the caravan to the bedroom. "Oh, fuck me drunk," he said as his eyes, getting accustomed to the dim lighting settled upon Roxy, dressed only in black lingerie, sprawled on the bed, huge tits barely held in a skimpy bra. Black stockings with lacy tops were held up by a black suspender belt, oh fuck, she hasn't got any drawers on, he thought.

Looking seductively at him she whispered, "I knew you'd come; I know you're a boob man." She rubbed her hands across her tremendous tits. She's hit the nail on the head there, he was a boob man but not those boobs, those boobs were trouble boobs and the last thing he needed right now was more trouble. He had to get out of there before she did anything else. Too late, Roxy rolled on her front and lifted her bare bum in the air, revealing her ample bottom. "See anything you like?" Roxy asked just as Dan caught a fleeting glance of Tina outside through a gap in the curtains. Dan let out a yelp.

"Is that you, Dan?" He heard Tina's voice outside, "Are you in there?" Dan leapt into the bedroom area and clambered across the bed. "Oh, slow down, sweetheart, we've got all day," Roxy murmured.

Dan clamped his hand across her mouth and hissed, "Shut the fuck up."

"So, you like a bit of rough stuff do you, that's ok with me." Roxy was up for everything, Dan was in danger of losing everything.

"Shut up, shut up, you silly slag, my wife's out there," he implored Roxy.

A thin caravan wall and a very thin piece of awning material were all that separated Tina from Dan and Roxy sprawled on the bed, Roxy in a state of undress and Dan in a state of sheer terror.

Roxy was reading the signals all wrong and reached for Dan's willy. An expert at todger liberation, in any state of erection from its owners' trousers, Dan's manhood was out. Dan tried to manoeuvre himself away and slipped landing on top of the rampant Roxy. "Oh, you like to keep your clothes on and do it," she purred. What was happening, Dan's mind raced. He came here to tell Roxy that she couldn't carry on her sexual encounters on his site and here he was knob out, lying on top of her and her huge tits, dressed only in stockings and a suspender belt.

Never being a particularly religious man in the past, Dan began to pray earnestly, "Please, please I beg of you, don't let Tina come in, I'll do anything, I'll give up alcohol, I'll go to church every Sunday, just don't let her come in."

So, he wants to keep his kit on and pray while doing it, Roxy catered for all types, but he was one of the weirdest.

Dan pulled himself free from Roxy's grasp and tumbled off the other side of the bed, laying on the floor, sweating, wide-eyed, wedding tackle out and anxious.

Was that Tina he could hear outside? Was she going to come into the awning? Was his life about to come crashing down, all because for once in his life he was trying to do the right thing, and for what? If this was what doing the right thing did for you, he'd make sure he never did it again. She must have seen his truck, Margaret Owens must have seen him and be telling Tina, "Oh I saw him go into that den of iniquity with that sordid harlot 20 minutes ago." He was done for. He peered over the bed; Roxy was now standing up and peeking through the curtain.

"It's ok, lover boy, she's gone." Dan slumped back on the floor in relief.

He had to get out of there, bugger the lecture, that could wait. He stood up, looking at Roxy, bugger they were magnificent tits, under any other circumstances who knows what would have happened, he thought.

Dan stood, not realising that his todger was still hanging limply from his trousers. "Get that done when you were in the army?" Roxy was staring at the face Dan had drawn on his todger. Dan looked down, completely forgetting his crude art form earlier in the weekend. "Army?" What was she on about?

Dan had to think quickly and get control over this situation. "Right, listen to me, Roxy, or whatever your bloody name is. I came here to tell you that if I hear you carrying on your 'business' on my site, you're out, you and that piss-head husband, immediate, gone, got it?"

Dan's message was clear enough, or so he thought.

"Not even if there's a freebie in it for you, say twice, maybe three times a week?" Roxy, standing with her hand on her hip was in a bargaining mood.

The thought of stirring all that porridge, sloppy seconds, maybe thirds, probably more, made Dan feel sick.

"I wouldn't go there if I was first in line, what the fuck is her fanny made of leather! All that action."

Dan walked out, turning to Roxy, "Don't push me on this, not on my site and Chris is onto you as well, so you'd better watch your step up there."

Roxy stared at Dan, "Well, he would be, he gets his freebies on Wednesday and the occasional Friday."

Dan shook his head and left, was everyone at it?

He sniffed his shirt, it wreaked of cheap scent, better get showered and changed, it's a dead giveaway.

Chapter 21: An Offer He Can't Refuse

The day had barely started, and Dan had had enough already. He'd sorted Roxy out and she wasn't under any illusion as to what would happen if she was caught entertaining on the site.

The police are bound to follow up on the terrorist fiasco the other day, so he had to make sure that there was none of Slav's contraband lying about on the site.

He hoped that Slav's Uncle Albertas had seen common sense and had told Slav not to keep any stuff here. He still needed a plan, talk was cheap and if Uncle Albertas didn't take no for an answer, he needed that 'thing,' a threat maybe, but not a physical threat, something that was a threat to his operation. But what?

He couldn't talk to Chris at The Seagull as he was in up to his neck. As Dan hadn't got a clue how to deal with Uncle Albertas, Slav and the rest of his criminal family, he needed someone who could, and that wouldn't be in the shape of the law.

Was that Joe's car outside his caravan? If it was, maybe he could come up with something. Dan knocked gingerly on the awning, hoping that Joe or Linda would hear. He was in luck; Joe opened the awning and beckoned Dan to come inside. "Coffee?" Joe asked. Linda made the coffee while Dan, yet again, went through his problems.

Joe listened. Dan went through everything in detail. When he had finished, he looked at Joe who had a hint of a smile on his face, which took Dan aback, didn't he believe him, for fuck's sake, don't tell me he's involved as well, why was he smirking?

Joe couldn't help it, he started to laugh, "So you want me to believe that you didn't know Roxy was on the game and that Slav and Irina weren't selling booze, fags and meat from their caravan, come on, Dan, you can't be that stupid, can you?" Dan obviously was, he did think that what he got from Slav, by way of the odd case or two of booze and the cartons of fags, was just that, the odd case. He felt stupid, ignorant, and no longer the player that he thought he was.

"So, what do I do, bugger the Roxy thing that's dealt with, it's Slav and his uncle I need to get sorted, but I haven't got a clue, I could get killed, or worse." Dan was in no mood for a lecture on his naivety.

Joe laughed again, "So, you think for smuggling booze, Slav and his uncle are killers, don't you think that it's not in their best interests to kill you, or anybody else, and just clear off and find a better place to hide the stuff, there must be 500 empty units along this coast." It was ok for Joe, he wasn't in the firing line, Dan thought. "I'll tell you what, get this meeting set up with his uncle and I'll come along as your Mr Big, we'll put them straight together."

Joe finished his coffee as Dan looked at him with relief and deep admiration. He would do this for me, what a mate he is.

The meeting was set for one o'clock in the afternoon. Dan called Joe, "Shouldn't we discuss tactics, a plan, what happens if they cut up rough, shouldn't they have shooters or something?" Joe's plan seemed suicidal as far as Dan was concerned, the plan was that Dan was to stay completely silent and deferent to him. He would do the talking and Dan wasn't to interrupt.

Sheer stupidity. Now Dan knew he was going to die.

Dan sat in his office, chain-smoking and staring at the clock. He was willing time to stand still. He saw Slav pull up outside and open the rear door for an elderly grey-haired man to get out. Was that Uncle Albertas? He was smartly dressed in a nice blue suit, no tie, a brilliant white shirt and well-polished black shoes. A big, but well-groomed moustache, neatly trimmed thick grey hair, a swarthy Mediterranean skin. No heavy overcoat draped across his shoulders, nobody kissing his hand, no armed heavies, Dan wasn't sure this could be the bloke, but he scared him shitless anyway.

They walked in, Dan had set out the chairs in his office making sure that none of them were opposite where Dan would sit behind his desk.

Dan's placing the chairs like this was so he was sure if the uncle or any armed heavies did that thing where they were concealing a revolver in their overcoat pockets, they couldn't shoot through the coat and blow off his bollocks.

They sat, Dan offered them whisky, they drank, no words were spoken, they sat in silence for a few moments waiting for Joe.

Joe pulled up alongside Slav's car and got out alone. The door opened and Joe walked in, Dan swallowed heavily. Joe fixed Uncle Albertas with a non-blinking stare. He turned to

Dan, without saying a word and made a firm hand gesture that signalled Dan to get out of the chair. Dan jumped up wishing that someone would say something, all this silence was going to get someone killed.

Joe leant forward, placing both arms on the desk and maintaining that fixed stare, "So tell me, Albertas, that is your name isn't it, what do you want to talk about?" His voice calm and measured; he sat back letting the question sink in.

Albertas finally spoke, "My nephew, Slav, he keeps some items, not bad items like drugs, good items, a few cases of booze, some smokes here and your man says no more, why he says that; we give him free items many times?" Dan went to speak but Joe cut him short.

"I don't want your stuff here, my stuff is already here, and you are shitting on my doorstep, and nobody and I mean nobody is shitting on my doorstep." Dan was on the verge of passing out, not Joe as well, what was Joe keeping here, more booze, more fags, wasn't anybody straight anymore, was everyone a bloody criminal.

Dan could feel the blood draining from his head.

Joe sat silently giving Albertas time to formulate a response. Albertas shifted in his chair, "So you have stuff here, booze stuff, drug stuff, what stuff?" He finished his question with a slight shrug of his shoulders. Joe stayed sat back in the chair, "That's my business, but it's not the same as your stuff and definitely, no drugs, so we're not competing against each other, so we don't need to fall out." He leant forward putting his arms on the table and fixed Albertas with that stare, "Do we?"

The air was filled with tension.

Oh shit, this is the point where the shooting starts, the panic and fear welling up inside of him made Dan fart. A long, clear, loud fart. Ffffrrrrtttttt, Fffrtt. Joe looked at Dan, Albertas and Slav also looked at Dan, and the smell of a thousand decaying rats filled the room. "Have you shit yourself?" Joe leant away from Dan, "That's fucking evil, what the fuck have you been eating?"

Dan looked sheepish, "Sorry, I'm err, not feeling well."

Joe stood up to put some distance between himself and Dan, "Not well, what have you got cancer of the arsehole, that's not normal, somethings died up your jacksy."

Dan shifted awkwardly in his chair letting another bottled-up fart go, Fffffffrrrrrttt, Fffrtt, Frrrttttt. It petered out, wetly.

Albertas whipped a clean white hanky from the breast pocket of his jacket and held it to his nose and looked at Slav, in Lithuanian he muttered, "Is this donkey's cock dying, he smells like a month-old Kibinai?"

Slav gagged unable to answer. Uncle stood up, thrust out his hand to Joe unable to stand another minute in that putrid atmosphere, "We go, only a little stuff, we move today, no need for fighting, Dan keeps his weekly stuff as a gesture from me, but Slav want to stay on-site, he liked Dan, cause no problems for him, ok?"

Joe, sharing uncle's willingness to depart the foul-smelling office stood up and shook uncle's hand, "Agreed."

Uncle and Slav left Dan and Joe in the office.

Joe turned to Dan, who was still sitting in his chair, "See, I told you that there wasn't any need to fret."

Dan smiled weakly. "Thanks, I thought I was going to die." Dan looked at him hunched in his chair.

His voice trembled on the verge of tears, he was sweating, smelly, and frightened, "Well, you smell like you died, that was the worst fart ever and who'd have thought farting could be such a forceful negotiating tool."

Dan looked at the floor, "I wish it was, I think I've shit myself, and what the hell are you storing here?"

The pair went outside into the fresh air, Joe reassured Dan that he hadn't got anything stored on the site, it was all a ploy, he bid Dan farewell and got in his car and left.

Dan stood alone, quietly taking in the site, the countryside, the hills, he was alive, the terrorist had fled, Roxy was under control, uncle was gone, and his worries were at an end.

He breathed in deeply through his nose making sure he was upwind of his stained trousers.

A car pulled up and a middle-aged woman in a short skirt and open top got out. Her legs were perfect, her bum was just as perfect and her, slightly, oversized breasts were temptingly exposed, "Got any space?"

Dan looked leeringly at her, "Of course, my dear, anything for a pretty lady."

He shuffled his now growing todger to one side.

Life, as Dan knew it, was returning to normal.